CURSED DIAMOND

DAVID GOUTCHER

ABOUT THE AUTHOR

David, is a former law enforcement officer who spent most of his career working under cover and in covert surveillance. He trained fellow officers in trade craft and survival skills and went on to work alongside UK Security Services. He also travelled abroad, liaising and collaborating with International Intelligence Agencies on covert operations.

Drawing from his experiences, he has created Spy Quest, an award winning, online interactive game which replicates the excitement and exhilaration that he found from real life missions. His first Spy Quest novel, co-written with Andy Briggs, is Polybius - The Urban Legend.

INTRODUCTION

Spy Quest is more than just a game.

Now you too can immerse yourself in the world of international espionage:
Join Sam, Rebecca, Casey and Holly in this action packed adventure as they follow the clues to solve the case of the Cursed Diamond.

Download the free Spy Quest app from iTunes for exciting additional augmented reality features:
Select 'Spy Cam', hold the camera over the illustrations within the book to receive intelligence updates and monitor targets with satellites in the sky.

Check out the list at the back of the book for locations to play the games. Follow us on Facebook and Twitter @SpyQuest for the latest news about upcoming books and events!

Now turn the page... and let the adventure begin!

IT'S NOT JUST A GAME...

Published in 2016 by Polybius Publishing
an imprint of Polybius Games Ltd
31 Clarkin Avenue, East Kilbride, G75 9GS
United Kingdom
www.polybiuspublishing.com

ISBN: 978-0-9932831-6-1

Printed and bound in Great Britain by Clays Ltd, St Ives plc

CONTENTS

Dedicated to my family and friends
who have helped me achieve
a lifetime ambition.

CHAPTER ONE
THE HEIST

"Stealth drones, activate!" murmured Franco under his breath. His drones needed only one command. A firm command and they would feed him the information, he needed.

Silent drones, whatever next... he thought, as his eyes slipped down to his arm; a holographic screen splayed before him, numbers and symbols were scrolling down the screen. The hologram bloomed into a video feed, that tracked the three other drones that he had initialised moments earlier.

The live video feed showed the drones in action. His eyes followed faint, glimmering little dots traveling all along the screen. A smirk tugged at the corner of his mouth.

A quick glance to ensure that they were working

properly and then back to securing the electric zip line. All was going to plan but time was of the essence.

It was a dry but cloudy night in Washington DC, the dark clouds above covered the glare of the moon. To most people, the eerie atmosphere on the rooftop would have sent a cold chill down their spine but Franco Rodriguez was no ordinary man.

The renowned International Jewel Thief had never been caught. Museum curators and art collectors around the world knew him only as "El Gato Oscuro," which meant "The Dark Cat." His daring exploits and ability to get around even the most sophisticated security systems struck fear into the hearts and minds of those in charge of protecting national treasures.

This heist wouldn't be any different from the last.

A final check before going past the point of no return. This was to be his most daring heist of all time. It is well known that the Natural History Museum had an alarm system to beat all alarm systems. Impregnable, they called it.

His prize, the Hope Diamond was located in a vault almost 200 feet below. It was protected by an expensive, sophisticated alarm system, 3 feet solid stone walls which were reinforced with iron girders and at any one time over 20 armed guards.

Franco didn't normally accept work for hire jobs but this was different. His unknown benefactors had provided some of the best technological gadgets that he'd ever seen; Stealth Drones that patrolled the night skies, each equipped with infrared high definition cameras and built in GPS. A hologram bracelet that displayed a live video feed and most important of all, a decoding machine that could hack into the door to the vault alarm system. The client also promised an inside man who would 'take care' of the sophisticated internal alarms systems. Without this, even he would have struggled to complete this mission.

He glanced down at his feet. Below him, he could see the shadows of the room settle around the exhibits. Although very dark, he had gotten used to seeing how shadows liked to fall around and beside display cases. His hologram bracelet relayed the path of his stealth drones, who were busy gathering information about the movements of the armed guards within. They locked onto heat signatures within and were able to feed this back to a 3D hologram of the museum, which appeared on his arm.

Carefully, Franco bent down, minimising the screen of his hologram bracelet.

Watching intently as the night guard walked below him. *Right on time*, he thought as he confirmed the time on his watch.

Quietly he placed the rubber suction pad in the middle of the large pane of glass and extended the four supporting arms out to the edge of the window frame. It was important that the arms were placed correctly to ensure that the circle of glass that he was about to cut, did not then fall down below. He also had to cut the glass as close as he could to the frame, so that the wire from the zip line would hold against the pressure from his body.

Franco steadied his feet, trying not to buckle too hard against the glass dome. He would soon know if the alarm to the roof had been disabled.

Taking in a deep breath he worked slowly, slicing the blade through the thick glass, till he could feel the window pane beginning to weaken under his pressure. The beads of sweat were forming on his brow. One more push of the blade and the thick glass pane, finally gave up its resistance. The wire arms immediately took the weight of the glass and held it in place.

He lifted the glass aside, to enable him to peer through the empty hole and as he predicted, it was large enough to allow him to slip through without a hitch. He'd made sure that the clothing he wore had been dark and tight enough to avoid malfunctions. Franco prepared himself, this is why he was hired!

Getting in the window was the easy part, from here on in, the success of the job would rely on his specialist skills and agility. He only had ten minutes before another guard would be walking by.

He gripped the cables before him, eyes traveling to the lip of the roof far on the other side of the building. There, the cables he had secured for the electric zip line also had an additional retractable cable set up for lowering himself into the vast room below. Franco pulled the cable, drawing more of the line toward him; enough that some pooled at his knees. Securing one end of the line around his waist and the loops of his utility harness, he carefully dangled his feet through the vacant hole. And then, he began his descent.

He had to be careful; if he shifted too much, or moved too little, the museum's sensors could go off in a matter of moments. A split second and his careful plans could unravel. Inch by inch, he lowered himself towards the floor.

A sudden unexpected noise from the far side of the room caused him to stop dead in his tracks. He knew that he was exposed but helpless to do anything about it. "Come on, come on!" He whispered as he peered agonisingly at the dark corner of the building from where the sound had come from.

After a couple of long moments, he completely dropped to a clear area inside the museum's highly secured rotunda.

Some distance away from him was a locked fire exit; secured from the interior of the museum. And, he was aware that it would potentially come in handy later.

His prize – the Hope Diamond, lay in the vault on the second floor. Like a cat, he regained his footing. The electric zip line had been drawn enough to hang low, but not too low. If he needed to reattach and zip back up to the roof, it would be hanging there, out of sight from the surveillance cameras quietly patrolling the area.

Franco started his trail toward the vault. Carefully, he manoeuvred around the display cases towards the stairway to the second floor, pausing in blind spots that he had initially plotted beforehand.

Weeks before, Franco had taken on a guise as a tourist. Innocent looking enough as he surveyed the carefully laid out artefacts and treasures defining the exhibits at the museum. Several blind spots had been littered around the hall. Lesser thieves would consider the blind spots unnecessary when he could just quickly rush through.

But Franco wasn't a lesser thief.

After moments, he managed to manoeuvre close enough to his target; a keypad that bore the lock securing the vault. According to his research, the vault's keypad had been reinforced against any force of nature. Any unstoppable force. But most things did have a weakness.

As he had practiced many times beforehand, he placed a small clear piece of film across the numerical keypad and then directed his gaze toward his wrist. He brought up his hologram again, finding the lock veiled in the screen's live infrared scanner. He could see where the visor had highlighted the lock's apparent weakness; the six digit number for the vault was the only numbers ever pressed on the keypad and his device had taken fingerprints from the pad and then identified which numbers they had pressed.

Instantaneously, it provided information about the numbers that formed the access code he needed to input. Franco tapped a few buttons on the screen and began the decoding process of inputing the numbers in the correct order.

The next stage was placing his hand on the adjacent security pad to enable it to verify his fingerprints. He knew how the device worked, within seconds it would replace his fingerprints with those that it had lifted from the numerical keypad. it would then fool the security pad into thinking it was the correct person entering the vault. He waited for the device's process to finish loading. His eyes bore down onto the fading screen.

The device finished and the door to the vault sprung open.

And there it sat: the Hope Diamond. The treasure had been concealed in a large, reinforced case. The clear top half of the case let in enough light to make the jewel absolutely shine.

Franco marvelled the prize for a quick moment, then held his breath; the moment of truth beckoned. The client that had hired him had guaranteed to kill the alarm on the case for several minutes. They had provided exceptionally detailed plans of the museum, and he had presumed that they must have someone in the control room who could switch the alarm off for enough time to let him take the diamond and replace it with a replica. Franco sniggered to himself as he thought about the curator looking at the diamond in years to come and realising that it was a fake. They wouldn't even be able to ascertain when the real diamond had been stolen. It was the perfect plan.

Another quick glance at his watch; he could feel the bead of sweat forming again on his forehead. 9:14 pm. 30 seconds to go.

That 30 seconds felt like an eternity, his heart was pounding and he was sure that had anyone been close by, then they would have been able to hear it from 100 yards away.

Finally, 9.15 pm. The hologram on his arm showed a live video feed from the drones that no one was anywhere near the vault.

He tentatively put his hand on the vault door and pulled it gently towards him.

It clicked open and Franco scooped up the prize with careful hands and slipped it inside his Cryptex, this was another personal device that he kept in his utility belt.

He took another few moments to restore everything back to the way he found it; everything except for his prize. Instead, the fake diamond now sat in its place.

A sudden vibration on his arm from the bracelet meant only one thing. DANGER. The screen immediately changed flashing a bright red, at the same time the sound of an alarm could be heard outside the chamber.

Franco gritted his teeth. He cursed to himself,

hearing the alarm blare throughout the building. He tried to close the door but heard the pitter patter of footsteps approaching him. He spun around fast and was startled to see a dark figure lunge at him. He lashed out with the torch in his hand and caught the person on the side of the head. The metal casing of the torch gave a sharp shock up his arm with the ferocity of the impact. The dark figure slumped straight to the floor with a loud crash.

Another dark figure came running toward him and he could hear the guards outside shouting.

"Secure the vault!"

He brushed past the second figure with ease and placed his hand in his pocket.

The room was filling with guards.

Franco understood how to improvise on the spot. His hand shot out, releasing a smoke bomb. It immediately detonated, billowing thick tufts of smoke into the stairway of the museum's second floor.

"He's getting away, search the smoke!"

"Argh, the smoke's too thick, I can't see a thing!"

"Keep searching; he can't have gone too far!"

Quickly he shot down the stairway and back to the ground floor. He threw another couple of smoke grenades in different directions, before he went to reattach the hooks.

Argh! One last thing, he thought, as he ran full pelt at the fire exit doorway. Smoke was billowing everywhere however, he knew exactly where to aim his leg. With a loud bang, the doors immediately sprung open under the force that he kicked the security bar with.

The muscles in his arms strained as he hoisted himself onto the electric zip line. Just briefly, he touched the bracelet on his wrist, controlling the device's mechanism, and closed the gap between the roof and the empty space of the museum's great hall.

As Franco balanced himself on the roof again, he spared himself a quiet chuckle. It hadn't been his first time escaping so quickly. But deep down, he felt as if his escape would lead him on a different path than his usual heist.

He steadied, gathering the electric zip line and dragged the trailing cable behind him. He quickly moved forward out of sight of the police that had begun surrounding the building.

They worked a lot faster than he thought.

He reached the opposite side of the building, where the lip of the roof framed his next destination. Franco took a long look down the side of the building and then across to the large area of grass opposite.

"Plan B" he murmured and then went to find the bag that he had secreted on the roof. His hands found their way to his shadow suit – as he called it. Franco wore fitted, darkened clothing for a reason. The shadow suit was actually a Wing Suit. Wing Suits had been specially designed for top-secret operations belonging to the world's most decorated covert organisations. Franco knew that the Wing Suit would come in handy; an operation of this type practically required one.

Quickly he slipped off his dark jacket and put on his suit. He made his way back to the edge of the building.

Franco crouched. He listened around. He didn't hear any more police nearby or below him, and the chopper patrolling the sky seemed to dart off into another direction. He smirked a little. *Looks like the decoy worked better than anticipated.*

Amid the smoke had been a hologram – a hologram of himself. The hologram had copied his mannerisms so well that others mistook the decoy for a human. The decoy device had been the one mechanism he took credit for, and he had been glad that he brought it along this mission. The security guards would have presumed that he had escaped through the fire door and would be searching the opposite side of the building from where he was going now.

Franco surveyed the area again; from down the alleyway, to the sky and even past the glass roofing below them.

The police weren't patrolling around the perimeter as far as he could tell.

Steadying his legs, he walked toward the edge of the building. As a skilled base jumper, scaling distances higher than 200 feet hadn't been an issue. Not when that had been the minimum for pulling off a successful base jump. He had the odds on his side and he wouldn't let things like the smallest margin of error get to him.

Franco jumped once more.

The wind beat through his Wings as he glided across the night sky. Gusts that flowed in and around his suit were perfectly suited for gliding tonight; the wind had been easy going, not blowing too hard or too soft. It also had been a chilly gust, which made cutting through the wind somewhat more pleasant than a more humid night. Franco followed the line of his shadow, and the grass before him, as he approached his landing spot.

The shock of landing shot through his legs for a moment. Then Franco regained his balance, dusted off his knees, and surveyed the area around him. His hand touched the Cryptex at his utility belt. He lightly patted the object. He has pulled off the stunt of a lifetime.

Franco consulted his bracelet again. He quickly brought up the hologram once more, hovering a finger above some of the buttons seen there. His eyes followed the holographic lines on the screen until he reached a set of buttons labeled with 'Stealth Drone Control.' Quickly, he pressed the biggest button on the screen, one that had controlled the main drone and waited for the drone to respond to his command.

Some distance ahead, the four drones he deployed earlier had been slowly hovering above the museum. They mainly surveyed the four corners of the museum and tucked high away from where security could find them. The main drone acted as a field leader. When Franco gave it directions; the drone responded and immediately lead the others to do what he needed the squad to do. This time, he needed the drones to return to their base. They belonged to the client and were preset with GPS co-ordinates so that they would return home. Franco didn't know where home for them was, but he'd been thankful for their help. He watched as they flew in formation away from his location.

Some distance away from the National Monument, and far enough away from the Museum, he had stashed the perfect getaway vehicle; his trusty motorbike. Franco retrieved his helmet which was hidden nearby, taking a moment to strap it on. Then he inserted his key into the ignition and started the bike. After a moment of the vehicle warming, he revved up its engine. After a brief moment of clarity,

Franco took off.

His mind was now racing and he was angry that

the client hadn't fulfilled their side of the bargain with the alarm system. He decided to keep to his plan and get out of town for a while, lie low, and wait till the heat had died down.

He drove straight to Ronald Reagan Airport.

Franco took a moment to take off his utility belt and the top portion of his Wing Suit. He swapped the jacket-like top for a shirt and tie, along with a simple coat. The Wing Suit was compact, and folding it into his bag was easy. After closing his bag, he straightened his clothing and hoisted his bag onto his shoulders.

Reaching into his bag. Franco unearthed his wallet and photo ID. Tucking the ID into his pocket with his wallet, he quickly walked down the airport parking lot and into the terminal building. He walked as fast as he could allow himself. But not too fast; he didn't want to rouse suspicious from passersby.

It took moments, but he arrived in the boarding area. The line progressed slowly, though. Even though a slow line had been the usual at the Ronald Reagan Airport, Franco couldn't wait any longer than another hour.

"Sir, your boarding card?"

Franco immediately looked toward the security guard. A plainly dressed woman nodded at him. He nodded back, reaching into his pocket. For a moment, he placed his bag down at his feet, before he handed over the boarding ticket and waited for the guard to check it over. Once they finished, they handed the item back. Franco tucked it back into his pocket, progressing through the line a little more after he picked up his bag again.

Sighing, he continued to move through the slowly disappearing line. He remained quiet, going through the motions of the airport security screening process. None of the airport security suspected him.

He didn't make eye contact as he removed his shoes and the appropriate items from his carry on, neither did any of the guards. After all, it had just been another day for all parties involved.

Gripping his carry-on bag, Franco placed it onto the airport scanner. He watched the bag travel up the conveyor belt; its contents revealed on the monitor ahead of him. One of the burly airport security guards looked at the monitor. His face took on a suspicious guise. Franco braced for the burly man's question.

He pointed at the monitor. "What's this?"

Franco looked at where he pointed. The burly man's finger hovered right where his Cryptex sat.

"Oh, that's just – that's just a kid's toy."

"A kid's toy?"

"It's a present for my nephew," Franco said, nodding. He kept his face neutral. "I bought it for his birthday. It's in a few days."

"Oh," the guard nodded, agreeing with him.

The burly man appeared satisfied with his story. Airport security likely heard the same story from other people already boarding the plane.

But they didn't know what really lurked within the present. The Cryptex was made of Brass and inside had been a hidden chamber. The chamber had been so precisely designed that it could get any precious item past security scanners with no problem. No one else could access the chamber, either. It could only be accessed by lining up the correct password, somewhat similar to a bicycle lock. And Franco had been the only person on the planet with knowledge of the password.

They finished checking the bag and allowed it to

pass through the security scanner.

"You're all set. You can take your carry on." Franco nodded and walked past the second security scanner. Fortunately, the alarm didn't go off.

At least, one alarm didn't trip during this operation, he thought as he reached for his bag.

"You have your passport, sir?"

"Oh, here," Franco reached into his pocket. He unearthed his passport and confidently handed it over to the guard behind the nearby desk. He regularly travelled with one of his many false passports. These were wise investments, as they had helped him travel anonymously and undetected to many countries worldwide.

"Thank you Mr Crosas" said the guard as he returned the passport.

Passing through airport security, after being cleared, Franco made his way quickly to the departure gate and finally boarded his plane.

He sat in his window seat, keeping his face tucked away from the other people on the flight. From what he could see, people were absorbed in their own business. For all they knew, he was just like them;

wanting to get to their destination as painlessly as possible. Franco didn't blame them.

An hour or so passed, as he waited for the plane to finally enter Florida. When he caught the familiar muggy trappings of the state, he let out a sigh of relief.

He had finally made it to Orlando and managed to pull it off. It was hard to believe that he had actually managed to escape with the Hope Diamond.

5
BREAKING NEWS ALERTS
SMITHSONIAN MUSEUM

CHAPTER TWO

BASIC TRAINING

"**O. M. G.**" cried Rebecca, "look at that. That looks so awesome." The excitement in her voice was at fever pitch.

Sam's attention was on the other side of the road, and he too stared with amazement at the huge 3D billboards at the side of the freeway.

Sam and Rebecca had never been to Orlando, Florida. The drive from the airport to their resort took them along the I4 freeway and past the Universal theme parks. Both sides of the road had massive 3D billboards advertising the latest attractions at the various theme parks in the state.

Visitors from around the world would have a hard choice choosing which park to go to, as there were so many wonderful things to do and see.

"There will be plenty of time for all that," said Agent Evans. "Lot's of hard work first, though."

Her words helped Sam to re-focus on why they were there.

After all of the excitement with Rebecca being kidnapped a couple of months ago, they had returned to the competition and their parents hadn't even realised that they had been missing.

Sam went on to win the competition and had gained entry to one of the world's finest pro-games team. Or at least, that's what they told their parents. In reality, both Sam and Rebecca had been accepted into the Spy Quest Agency, and their cover story for missions and training would be that they would be attending professional games competitions around the world. Sam would be the contestant and Rebecca allowed to travel with him for company.

Agent Evans had collected Sam and Rebecca from the airport and was taking them to the training camp. This was the first time they had met anyone from the agency since the competition.

Sam studied their driver. She seemed to have a kind, warm personality; the kind of person who would be your favourite auntie.

Agent Evans could obviously feel Sam's stare and turned towards him. "That's us here."

Sam looked out of his window and could see that the billboards advertising the theme parks had been replaced with adverts for the shopping outlets.

"WOW!" He exclaimed, "I think, every well-known designer brand has an outlet in there."

"Yes, it's nice and handy for those of us that like shopping," Agent Evans said with a smile.

Agent Evans turned the opposite direction and entered a private road which led to a set of security gates. The guard waved to Agent Evans and opened the gates without having to say anything.

Palm trees lined the sides of the street and holidaymakers wandered around with their inflatables and towels.

"Welcome to our little bit of paradise," Agent Evans said. "Let's get you checked in and then we can take you on a tour of the resort."

With a word of warning she added, "Remember, the resort is a cover for our training camp, most people here are on their vacation and have no idea that this is a Secret Spy, training camp."

"We all live in apartment blocks within the main resort and your next door neighbours will be fellow Agents however, families on their vacation may wander through too."

The check-in pavilion was enormous. Queues of people waited patiently in line with their suitcases by their side. Excited children ran about the hall and members of the children's team were trying to entertain them long enough to take the pressure off their tired parents, who had been travelling for hours and now just wanted to get their keys and get settled into their villa.

Agent Evans led them by the queue's and out of the opposite side of the building, into the resort.

"Jump aboard," she instructed, as she sat in a golf buggy. "We use these electric buggies to get around the resort."

Sam and Rebecca placed their bags in the luggage holder at the back of the buggy and jumped in. The resort was beautiful with lush green grass and small lakes with fountains in the middle, positioned between the villas and apartment buildings.

Agent Evans handed them both a small black band which was similar to the silicone bands worn by guests who had booked an all inclusive holiday.

"These are your 'Cecret' bands" they will grant you access to the restricted areas of the resort and even open the door to your apartments."

"Wear them at all times," she added.

Agent Evans left them to get settled in and told them to report to the activity centre at 6 pm sharp.

"Spider… Arghh, it's crawling over your leg!" Screamed Rebecca.

Sam jumped up as though he'd been woken from his sleep by a huge volt of electricity.

"Where, where?" He exclaimed.

"Gotcha," laughed Rebecca. She knew that Sam had a terrible fear of Spiders.

"Hurry up, we're going to be late," she said, as she threw Sam his sunglasses box.

Both of them hurried out of the apartment. The sun was still lovely and warm, but the humidity had eased slightly.

Sam used his mobile phone to follow the GPS

map which directed them to the activity centre.

It was good to see a familiar face waiting outside the activity centre.

"Late as usual, I see," said Agent Jones, with a wry smile.

He welcomed them both with a warm embrace.

"Good to see you both. How was your flight?"

Sam and Rebecca both started to ramble with excitement about all the wonderful things that they'd seen already.

"Haha, yes, the theme parks are fabulous, and we will make sure that you get a chance to see them but first let's get you introduced to your buddies and have a look around."

They all jumped on a nearby buggy, and Agent Jones drove them to the far side of the resort. Along the way, he pointed out the various restaurants, convenience stores, cafe's and pool decks in the resort.

As they approached large gates at the edge of the resort, Agent Jones stopped the buggy and walked to the gates. He placed his hand on a danger sign that warned of alligators. The gates suddenly swept open.

On the other side of the gates, the tarmac road

stopped and turned into a dirt track leading through a thick forest and horrible looking swamp. Even in daylight, it looked very eerie.

Agent Jones jumped back aboard the buggy and continued through the gates. He warned them both that Florida was famous for its swamps and alligators.

"Alligators are considered an endangered species and therefore protected by the government. They live wild and have been known to snatch dogs and young children who ventured too near to the edge of the lakes and swamps."

"So be careful next to water." He added, with a nod of the head which was to reaffirm the seriousness of his statement.

The dirt track only lasted a hundred yards and then changed back to a proper road and what appeared to be an extension of the holiday resort. The buildings were the same but assault courses replaced the pool decks and shops.

Groups of teenagers wearing similar coloured t-shirts were busy climbing over the walls in an assault course, and others were scaling a huge climbing frame in the centre of the grass.

They made their way to a large building in the centre. It appeared similar to the reception building. However, everyone was similarly dressed and wearing uniformed t-shirts rather than holiday clothes.

Agent Jones led them through the building to an open area, which had a billiards table; arcade game machines lined up along the wall, and a large wall mounted TV.

An older boy and girl were playing an arcade machine in the corner. They turned when they heard them approaching, and their faces lit up when they saw Agent Jones.

Agent Jones introduced everyone, “Sam, Rebecca, I’d like to introduce you to Casey and Holly.”

“They will be your Buddy mentors for your first six months of training.”

They all exchanged handshakes, and Rebecca could feel her face feeling a bit flushed as Casey shook her hand.

“Buddies are SQA Agents who have more experience and are assigned to new recruits so that they can help them settle in” explained Agent Jones.

“I’ll leave you to get acquainted.”

"Show them around the camp guys and I'll see you all at 9 am sharp tomorrow morning," said Agent Jones before he headed off.

Casey acted as tour guide and led everyone around the training camp. The first stop on the tour was back outside at the assault course.

"This is 'Death Valley', otherwise known as the assault course."

"Everyone trains here at least once a day," added Casey as he gave an impish stare at them.

Holly saw the look of fear in Sam and Rebecca's eyes and tried to allay their fears.

"Don't worry, it's not as bad as it looks and the instructors don't push you like it's the military."

"Everything here is fun to do." She gave Casey a punch on the arm for pulling their legs.

"Casey is a natural athlete and loves this course, but watch the fear in his eyes when you ask him to do the mental agility," she added with a wink at Sam.

Casey cut her short by explaining why everyone was wearing different coloured t-shirts.

"Agents earn their colours by how many missions they've been on, you can tell how experienced an Agent is by the colour of their t-shirt."

Holly added, "the system is similar to the grades in martial arts. You've been given your Black t-shirt and a White one, everyone wears the Black t-shirts when they are in a live operation but obviously not when you're actually working undercover, and you wear the White one when you are here on camp for training. After completing two missions, you will earn an Orange one, three missions - Sky Blue, four missions - Green, five missions - Red, six missions - Yellow and seven missions - Royal Blue."

Rebecca chipped in with "Why do you wear Black t-shirts with Special Agent written on it?"

"We've completed over eight missions," said Holly.

"That's when you earn Special Agent status and then you just wear Black t-shirts."

The four of them had been that busy in conversation as they walked that Sam didn't realise that they had covered so much ground and were now standing beside a huge dome shaped hanger.

Casey held his bracelet against a pad on the door and waited till he heard the click of the lock before pushing a button at the side. The heavy door slid open, and Casey beckoned them all to follow him in.

Sam was immediately in heaven.

The circular building had three floors, and each level had monitors on the exterior walls with Gamers busy playing a variety of games on different consoles. In the centre of the ground floor was an array of computer simulator machines. The machines were in action and crowds of Agents gathered around monitors next to each machine, to watch what was happening within the machine.

"I can't wait to get started in here," Sam whispered to Rebecca.

Sam looked around to see that Rebecca had wandered off behind Casey.

"Ah, that will be the Casey effect," Holly said to Sam.

"Blond hair, Blue eyes, and a figure an Olympic athlete would be proud of, girls find him irresistible," she said as a matter of fact.

"Huh, he's welcome to the Nerdinator," retorted Sam.

The quizzed look on Holly's face showed that she hadn't heard the word "Nerdinator" before.

Sam and Holly quickly caught up with Casey and followed him out of the dome and through a corridor to a large gym hall. Agents were split into small groups within the hall.

"This is where you will train in the distinct styles of ancient martial arts," said Casey.

"Do we still use the Polybius games to teach us the moves?" Asked Sam.

"Yes, the Polybius games will continue to enhance the speed in which you learn but you will still need to practice the physical side of the arts too," replied Casey.

He continued walking at pace and pointed out a large indoor pool which formed part of the same complex. They exited the building and Sam was surprised to see that they were back at the main office. The tour was over, and they all headed back to the main resort to get them settled in.

Over the next few days Sam and Rebecca tried everything from Archery, Drone flying, and the assault course, to Judo, Karate and Ju-Jitsu. Sam's favourite was naturally the gaming experience. The simulators were designed to be as close to the real thing as possible and Sam couldn't stop talking about the exhilaration he felt from flying planes across photo-realistic landscapes and driving supercars across mountain terrains and riverbeds.

Rebecca was thankful for the help from Casey and Holly. They had made her feel very welcome and although she didn't like the physical side of the camp, she appreciated that they never pushed her beyond her limits. She regarded Holly as the big sister that she had never had and liked when they got some time together to just sit and chat.

Sam had tried to match Casey on the assault course and had been left trailing every time.

"I'm sure that Casey has had too much exposure to the Polybius chip," said Sam to Rebecca as they headed out to meet with Casey and Holly at the recreation room.

"Why's that?" Rebecca replied.

"He's like a supercharged Robot on steroids. He never tires."

Rebecca laughed. "You are jealous!"

"No," retorted Sam.

"Holly told me that Casey has had a hard time recently, so go easy on your assumptions," said Rebecca.

"What's wrong with him?" Said Sam, a bit too loudly.

"What's wrong with who?" Came a familiar voice from behind them.

Neither of them had heard Casey coming up behind them.

The look that Sam and Rebecca gave each other, revealed that they were talking about him.

"I guess you were talking about me which means that Holly has told you why we're stuck here at the training camp," said Casey.

Rebecca was about to defend Holly for telling her but Casey stopped her.

"It's okay, I'm fine now and I hope to be back operational within the week."

Sam was bemused, "What happened, are you alright?"

"I'm fine now. I was on a live mission and got

knocked out just as I was about to catch a thief in the middle of a big robbery."

"Tell me more," said Sam.

Over the last few days Casey had been telling him about some of the missions that they'd been on and Sam loved hearing the tales of his daring exploits.

"Recently, Holly and I have been seconded to a special ops team. Its remit is to protect the world's treasures."

They had just reached the recreation area and Rebecca could see that Sam was totally hooked on every word from Casey. She went to order drinks whilst the boys grabbed a seat.

Casey went on. "We travel the world to find lost treasures, prevent robberies and even track down stolen artefacts that are now in private collector's hidden collections." Casey loved telling new recruits about his experiences and continued.

"We have taken part in archaeological digs and even deep sea diving for sunken ships and treasure."

"What went wrong with the robbery?" Asked Sam.

His intervention cut Casey's story short.

"Our specialist Source Unit had an untried informant give us information about a daring heist at the Smithsonian National Museum of Natural History in Washington."

"The source gave us details on an International Jewel Thief that we have been trying to catch for years."

"Holly and I had been hiding beside the vault that contained the Hope Diamond and sure enough the thief managed to get by the security and was just taking the diamond when we surprised him."

"Just as I lunged to tackle him, he turned and hit me on the side of the temple," "Knocked me clean out."

"I was out for a full week and in a coma."

"I've been on light duties for six weeks now and hope now to get the all clear to resume normal duties."

Sam's eyes were widening as Casey described how they had hid beside the vault for hours before the Thief was due to break in.

"What happened to the Thief and the Diamond?" Asked Sam.

Casey beckoned him to come closer and spoke in a hushed voice.

"The trail to find him went cold here."

Casey could see the puzzled look on Sam's face and went on.

"We discovered that he flew to Orlando straight after the Heist and that's why I volunteered to come to this training camp for my light duties."

His demeanour changed from talking secretive about the operation to someone with an obvious determination to catch their man.

"I want to be close by when we finally locate him."

Casey then added with a sense of certainty, "I know he's still here, I can feel it."

SUSPECT LOCATED
WANTED
REWARD $5,000,000
FRANCO RODRIGUEZ
FRANCO RODRIGUEZ
ORLANDO INTERNATIONAL AIRPORT

CHAPTER THREE

BRAKKER

"BANG," BANG," "BANG."

Sam and Rebecca both came staggering out of their rooms at the same time. It was the middle of the night.

"What on earth is that?" Said Rebecca.

"It sounds as though someone is trying to kick the door in," replied Sam.

"Sam, wake up, It's only me," came the familiar voice from the other side of the door.

"Casey!" Said Sam in bewilderment.

"Yes, hurry up and open the door," came the reply.

Sam had hardly unlocked the door and Casey barged in, nearly knocking him over in his hurry to get in the room.

"I told you, I told you," he kept repeating in between excitedly telling Sam and Rebecca to get changed quickly.

"Casey! It's only 4 am," said a very tired Rebecca.

Casey turned to Rebecca who was heading to her room again and pleaded with them both, "Franco, he's here! And I need your help to catch him."

Sam had already relayed the story about the Heist of the Hope Diamond to Rebecca and she was well aware of who Franco was and why Casey would be so excited to have found where he was.

They both got ready as quickly as they could and Casey started to fill them in on the recent developments.

After the Heist, Franco had indeed flown to Orlando. The following day, the FBI had used the GPS signal on Franco's cell phone to locate it within Orlando airport arrivals gate. It was found discarded in a waste bin. Analysis of the last call made from it had indicated that he'd made an international call to a Dutchman called Kriss Brakker. At the time of the call, Brakker was in Amsterdam, Netherlands.

The Spy Quest Agency had asked Interpol to assist with intelligence on Brakker.

"I've just had an update from Interpol. Over the last few days, Brakker has been calling an unregistered cell phone which has been located here in Orlando." He paused for a moment, half expecting to hear a 'WOW' or something from Sam or Rebecca. But they just stared back at him with tiredness in their faces.

He continued, "an Interpol surveillance team followed Brakker to Schiphol airport a few hours ago and he boarded a flight to Orlando."

"He's coming here and I'll bet that he's going to meet with Franco."

Sam didn't want to share his thoughts with Casey but whispered to Rebecca. "Is it just me or could 2+2 be making 5 here?"

Rebecca nodded in agreement. Both of them had become very friendly with Casey and were happy to help in any way they could. Even if it did prove to be a false lead.

They locked up and the three of them joined Holly in a waiting limousine outside the apartment.

"To the airport please driver," said Casey.

Sam stared at the driver. He wasn't your typical looking limousine driver. Sam gave himself a shake - how would he know what a typical limousine driver would look like, he'd never been in a limo before.

Rebecca had the same feeling about the driver. He was big and looked mean. She kept catching him looking in the rear view mirror and felt a sense of unease about his constant questions.

"Aren't you kids a bit young to be going to the airport on your own?" The driver asked.

"We're meeting our father there," replied Holly.

"Going to surprise him," added Casey.

Sam was amazed at how quick they came back with an answer to the driver. Sam and Rebecca smiled at each other, both of them impressed at how good their buddies were.

Rebecca decided to play the driver at his own game and test her new skills. Every time he looked in his rear view mirror, she would strain her neck slightly upwards, as though she was making a mental note of his appearance.

It worked better than she thought it would. The driver put his sunglasses on and stopped turning his head to look in the mirror. She nudged Sam in his ribs and nodded towards the driver.

Sam had seen the driver putting his sunglasses on and had thought it a bit weird, as it was the middle of the night.

The driver didn't speak for the rest of the journey.

The limo stopped outside the Arrivals doors, and they all jumped out.

"Do you want me to wait here for you?" Queried the driver.

"No, thanks," said Sam before Casey could say anything.

They all made their way into the terminal building and scanned the arrival's board to see when the plane from Schiphol arrives.

"Right, we have another hour before he arrives, take these," said Holly as she handed them all a pair of sunglasses.

"Before you ask, they're not your usual sunglasses," added Casey.

"Let's find a quiet place to have a seat and try them out," said Holly as she headed off to a seated area at the corner of the building.

The male glasses were slightly different from the female one's and had a different designer logo on the side of each.

"Blink three times quickly," said Holly in a hushed voice.

"OMG! That's amazing," said Rebecca as a small digital screen appeared on the inside of her glasses.

Sam quickly put his glasses on and tried the same.

"Wow!" He murmured.

Holly continued. "The glasses will only work for you, they are paired to work with your 'Cecret' band. They have full internet access and are linked to headquarters at all times."

Holly made sure that everybody's glasses were working properly before giving instructions on how to use them.

"You can use voice instructions or eye movements to control the content you see," she added.

Casey went to get all of them a drink and a quick bite of breakfast, while Holly helped them both to get to grips with the glasses.

It took over half an hour for Sam and Rebecca to get the hang of how to control the eye movements.

Casey returned and handed out the foods and drinks to everyone.

"I'm sending everyone an intelligence file on everything that we have so far in the case."

Immediately, a Red dot appeared at the top right hand side of Sam's peripheral vision. He looked at the dot and blinked twice quickly. Instantly a screen appeared and a video with a case file called the 'Cursed Diamond' started playing.

It showed the latest photograph of the main suspect Franco Rodriguez, pictures taken from within the vault at the museum after the robbery and the incriminating fingerprint evidence linking Franco, which was taken from the roof of the museum building. There was also a recent photograph of Kriss Brakker.

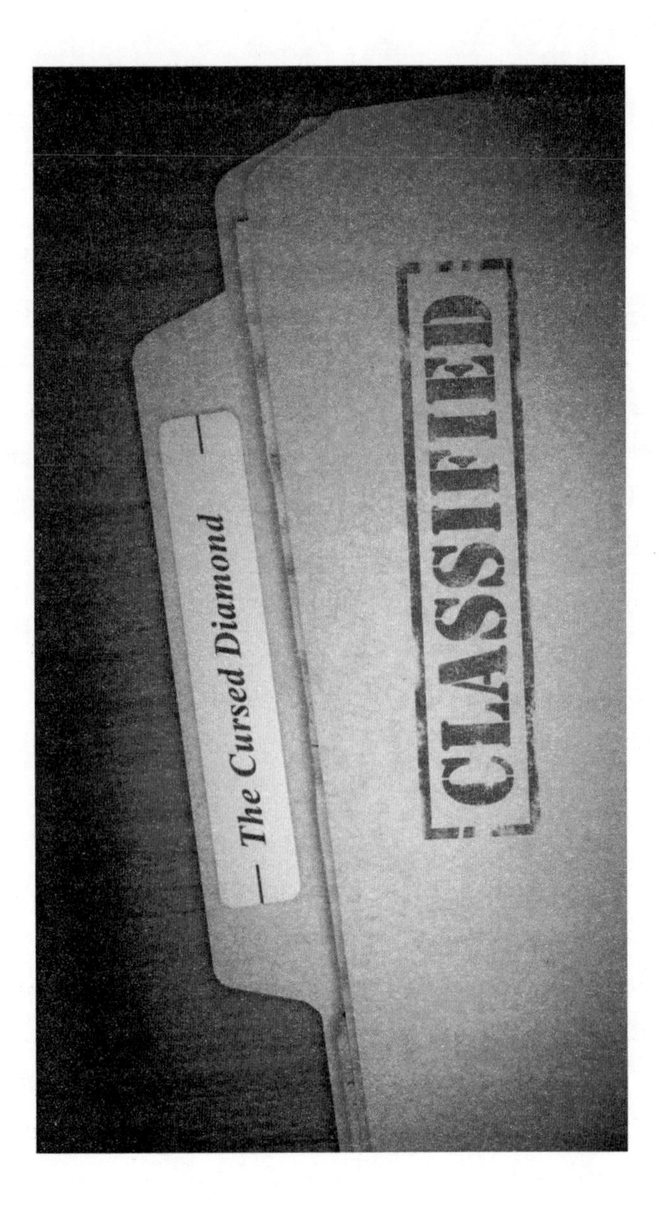
The Cursed Diamond
CLASSIFIED

"Your glasses have built-in face recognition," said Holly after giving everyone enough time to view the file. She then gave instructions on how to access the scanning mode for face recognition.

"Rebecca, I want you to be the lookout at the doorway at the arrivals door," said Casey as he pointed over to a set of double doors which led from the secure airport side to the main airport terminal.

"Sam, this is your chance to put the surveillance theory you've been taught into practice, as the rest of us will form a standard three-man team and on Rebecca's signal, we will follow Brakker."

Holly and Sam nodded in agreement.

"Rebecca, when we leave, you will be responsible for getting us a Limo and picking us up if Brakker enters a car."

"Why a Limo?" She asked.

"Private limos are quite common at the airport and costs a bit more to hire, but families that come to Orlando are willing to pay a bit more for what is usually a never to be repeated holiday of a lifetime."

"The advantage for us is that we can't be seen within it and the driver can't hear what we are saying, as we can turn off the intercom and close the privacy window" replied Casey.

"Okay, put your earpieces in and let's get to our positions."

Rebecca headed over to the crowd of people who were gathered around the arrival's door. Private limousine drivers were holding cards bearing the surnames for expectant business travellers who would be whisked away to their meetings. Many others were apparently waiting for family members who they probably hadn't seen in a while.

She positioned herself so that she would get a view of everyone's face as they approached her.

Rebecca could feel her stomach churning. This was the first time she had been left on her own as part of a covert operation. The last few months had been a blur, and she still had to pinch herself on everything that had happened. Her stomach started to convulse, and she could actually feel a bit of sickness coming up the back of her throat.

"Pull yourself together," she whispered.

Rebecca had insisted on joining Sam as an Agent and her ability to finish the Polybius game on Sam's mobile and calmness when she had been kidnapped, had convinced Agent Jones that she would be an excellent asset.

"I'm not going to mess this up, I'm not going to mess this up," she kept repeating.

Luckily, the family next to her were all speaking excitedly in Spanish and didn't appear to understand her mutterings.

After what seemed an eternity, the doors opened and a man similar to Brakker walked towards her.

"Standby, Standby, Standby," she whispered.

The screen on her glasses suddenly jumped into life. Crosshairs centred on Brakker's face and numerous points started appearing with a loading bar at the bottom.

Within a split second, the words 'Identity Confirmed' appeared across the centre of the screen.

"Target confirmed," she whispered.

"Roger, game on!" Said Casey to confirm that he had heard her.

"Roger," said Sam and Holly in sequence.

Rebecca stood her ground and watched as Brakker walked right by her and towards the exit.

She moved to a quieter area away from the crowd and gave a running commentary on Brakker's direction and description of his clothing.

As he disappeared from view, she heard Casey take up the commentary on his movements.

"Phew," Rebecca exclaimed in relief. Her first task as an Agent had gone smoothly.

She hurried in the opposite direction to find a private Limo.

Brakker headed straight from the terminal building and followed the signs for the car hire rentals. The three-man team changed over surveillance duties with the precision of an experienced team. It was Sam's turn to get close to him in the Hertz car rental office and he watched as a female assistant took him over to a large Silver coloured SUV which was in the Hertz parking lot, alongside what looked like a sea of different size, shape and coloured cars that were waiting on someone hiring them.

The female assistant then walked away from Brakker back towards the office and Sam gave a running commentary as Brakker entered the driving seat of the car.

Brakker began pulling out of the line of cars and Sam turned to make his way to the Limo.

"Wait! Someone else is approaching Brakker!" Sam said sharply. He had turned back to give Brakker one more watchful glance and had been caught by surprise.

He returned to his original position to watch what the male with a high visibility vest was going to do. As he peered at the male, he suddenly realised that the unknown male was, in fact, Casey.

Casey! What are you doing? Thought Sam, as he watched Casey walk behind Brakker's car.

Bakker pulled away completely unaware that Casey had passed by the rear of his car.

"Rebecca, meet us at the bus stop outside departures!" Shouted Casey as he ran from the parking lot."

Rebecca was waiting in position with a private limo and had already closed the privacy glass.

They had hardly shut the doors with them all inside when Sam blurted out, "are you crazy, he could have seen you?"

" What were you thinking of?"

Casey looked at him with a stare of a disapproving master to his upstart of an apprentice.

"I placed a tracker on his car and had to get close enough to put it on the rear of the vehicle without alerting him," he replied in a stern voice.

"Ah! Sorry," said Sam in a sheepish voice.

The four of them could view the tracker on the screen within the glasses, but Sam was beginning to feel it hurting his eyes a bit and took his own off. Holly instructed Rebecca to take her's off too and Casey used the intercom button to direct the limo driver to where they were going.

Brakker was approximately half a mile ahead of them and headed towards the theme parks. In the distance, Sam could see from the dark clouds that they were headed towards a tropical storm. The Floridian climate was very much a tropical one and hardly a day passed by without an hour or so of torrential rain.

The interior of the car began to darken and without any warning a huge crack of thunder could be heard right above the car. Rebecca moved a little closer to Sam.

"Is that normal?" She asked.

Forked lightning continually lit up the interior of the car. It was her first time in a car when a storm had hit, and they appeared to be driving straight into the eye of the storm.

"Don't worry, it's perfectly normal," said Holly in a calming voice. She took Rebecca's hand and gave it a gentle squeeze.

Within ten minutes, they had driven straight through the worst of the storm and were now out of the other side.

"You wouldn't even guess that it had been raining," said Sam as he peered out of the car at the ground below.

The heat of the sun quickly dried the rainwater up, and local people were glad that it also helped to reduce the humidity as well.

"I think he's arrived at his destination," said Casey.

Everyone put on their glasses and could see that the tracker was now stationary within a holiday resort complex in Lake Buena Vista.

They instructed the driver to stop outside the complex so that they could all enter on foot.

"Better that we split up. Holly, you take Rebecca and search the nearby poolsides, shops, and restaurants for any sign of Franco. Use your Face Recon to help you."

Holly nodded in agreement.

"Sam and I will find where Brakker is and watch his apartment."

Both parties split up before they entered the resort.

"Nobody will ever suspect children of being spies," Casey told Sam. "Just relax and remember to act as though you are on vacation,"

It was now 10 am and holidaymakers were shuffling back and forward from their apartments to pool decks and restaurants. The smell of cooked sausages filled the air as Casey and Sam searched for Brakker's car.

The Lake Buena Vista resort was just as large as the Vistania and had a variety of villas and apartments. Luckily, car parking spaces were all marked to correspond with whichever villa or apartment you were staying in; so it should be quite easy to identify where Brakker was.

The tracker led them straight to the vehicle. Sam marvelled at it's accuracy, as the GPS signal was accurate to a few metres.

The SUV was parked and unattended outside a detached villa, which had its own driveway.

Casey and Sam found a good vantage point from the front of an ice cream parlour which was diagonal across the street. Two old-fashioned wooden rocking chairs on the wooden decking of the shop offered the perfect viewing location. From there they could see the front door and side of the villa, as well as the only entrance to the street for any vehicles.

Holly and Rebecca searched all the nearby restaurants, shops, and pool decks but could find no trace of Franco.

"Time to get some sun," Holly said with an impish smile.

She picked up a couple of bath towels from beside the pool deck and put them out on two sun loungers next to the pool.

She slipped out of her shorts and t-shirt and had a bikini underneath.

"Always come prepared," she laughed as she got

comfy on the lounger.

"But! I don't have a change," said Rebecca.

"You're a trained Agent! You'll think of something," replied Holly.

Rebecca looked around and quickly understood what Holly meant.

The poolside shop sold everything from swimming costumes to inflatables. She went over and bought the cheapest bikini that they had and a bottle of sun protection lotion.

Within ten minutes, she returned to lie beside Holly.

Without saying as much to each other, they both thought that perhaps Casey's assumption that Brakker was here to meet with Franco was a bit hopeful on his part.

A couple of hours past and nothing happened.

The girls were enjoying lying basking in the midday sunshine, and the boys were on their fourth milkshake.

Sam decided to share his concerns.

"Do you think there's a chance that Brakker isn't here to meet with Franco?"

"I don't believe in coincidences," retorted Casey.

Casey appeared to be in another world for a few moments and then shared his thoughts on why he was sure that Brakker would lead them to Franco and ultimately to the Diamond.

"Brakker was the last person that Franco spoke to before he threw away his cell phone. I believe that he was telling him that he'd escaped and that he was going to lie low for a while."

He looked over at Sam, "It's the only explanation that makes sense."

Sam could think of a couple of other scenarios but decided against sharing them.

Cars and vans came and went from the street. Holidaymakers came and went from the Ice Cream parlour, and still, nobody came to the door of the villa. Sam decided to rest his eyes and before long was fast asleep.

He woke suddenly with Casey shaking his arm.

"What's up?" Sam muttered as though he'd been awake the whole time.

"That SUV has been down the street twice and circled the road a few times as well." Casey nodded towards a Black coloured Porsche SUV that was now parking on the street outside the villa.

"Come on, Come on," whispered Casey under his breath.

His hopes that Franco was about to get out off the SUV were soon dashed as a male and female got out of the vehicle.

They both gave a suspicious glance around them as they walked up the driveway towards the front door. The door opened just before they reached it and Brakker could be seen beckoning them both to come inside.

"Wait here and keep your eyes on the front for any movement" Casey ordered Sam. He then ran off towards the side of the villa next to Brakker's.

"Casey!" Sam called aloud.

Casey made sure that his movement could not be seen from the house. He had already picked the best way to get to the villa without being seen and had taken the opportunity as soon as it presented itself. He moved from the front of each villa till he was outside Brakker's window. Crouched down, he moved to underneath the front window.

Sam watched him edge closer and muttered, "what on earth are you doing?"

Holly had warned Sam and Rebecca that Casey could sometimes be a bit GungHo and act without thinking about things first. This definitely seemed to be one of those times.

The girls had heard the commotion and got themselves ready.

Casey listened with intent outside the window. He could hear raised voices and the occupants were clearly having an argument about something.
Sam's earpiece crackled with a message from Casey.

"Sam, can you take the tracker off Brakker's vehicle and put it on the Porsche?"

"Where are you going?" Replied Sam.

"I'm going to try and get a better look at what's going on from the rear of the villa," came the reply from Casey.

Sam watched as Casey disappeared around the side of the building.

He then followed Casey's path as he tried to get to the front of the villa.

Brakker's car was easy to get to without being seen.

Sam found the tracker with ease. To most people, it would look like a small bird poo but it contained a powerful transmitter. It felt horrible and squashy in his hand as he peeled it off.

"Yuk," Sam murmured.

This was the dangerous bit. How could he be sure that no one was watching from the villa.

Instead of crouching, he stood tall and walked purposely towards the rear of the Porsche. He thought it would only make him more suspicious if he was seen crouching as he made his way there.

Once behind the trunk door, he waited with baited breath. He could feel his heart racing madly. Had anyone seen him. It would only be a matter of seconds till he'd know for sure. He waited for the sound of the front door to fly open and got ready to run.

Nothing happened.

"Casey. Come in. Can you hear me?" Came Holly's voice over the earpiece.

"I think we've found him."

The excitement in Holly's voice meant only one thing. They'd found Franco!

LIVE CCTV FEED
INCOMING CALL TRACE
AMSTERDAM, NETHERLANDS

CHAPTER FOUR

THE RUSSIAN CONNECTION

Casey abandoned his position and was creeping around the side of the villa. Looking underneath the car he could see Sam's feet at the other side.

Just then, he heard the front door of the villa open.

He jumped back against the wall.

The argument between the occupants of the car and Brakker continued to the doorway.

Casey could hear them more clearly now and was sure that the both of them were Eastern Europeans, maybe even Russian.

They clearly weren't happy with Brakker and in broken English were making him know exactly how they were feeling.

Casey jumped over the fence and into the

garden next door.

He could get a better view of everything from there and use the garden foliage to try and get a photograph of the two of them as they left.

"Tomorrow, NO LATER!" Barked the unknown male at Brakker.

With that, the two of them walked back to their car.

Casey managed to get a side photograph of both of them before they got into the car. Unfortunately, it wasn't enough of a profile for the face recognition to identify them.

Casey's thoughts suddenly turned to the whereabouts of Sam.

"Sam, come in."

"Sam, come in. Where are you?" The alarm in Casey's voice was evident.

Rebecca was trying not to get worried. She had Franco in her sight and was trying to concentrate on his movements.

There was no reply from Sam.

Casey could feel his throat drying and a sense of fear creeping in. His mind was racing.

Where could Sam have gone? He replayed the events in his head.

He would have heard them shout if they'd seen him. The last place he had seen Sam was at the back of the SUV.

Casey's screen then showed a message,

"Incoming Message from Sam."

The message read "I'm in their SUV."

Oh, No! thought Casey.

Sam must have heard them coming and panicked. He'd jumped into the back of their car and was now trapped there.

"Sam, I realise that you can't speak, I've got your message and I'm on my way to help you."

Casey then instructed the girls to continue to watch Franco and he would follow Sam.

Transport, he thought as he scanned the area looking for a suitable vehicle. He switched the glasses onto the tracker mode and immediately the tracker showed the location of Sam.

Casey ran over to the Ice Cream Parlour and started trying to open the doors of the cars parked there.

"Click" *hey presto*, he thought as the door opened. Casey had been taught how to hot wire a car, and although he was legally underage, he was already an experienced driver. Well, at least on simulators.

Casey had the car started in seconds and was off in pursuit of Sam.

Driving the car in real life was no different from the sims.

The large open roads in Orlando helped him to catch up with the Porsche quite quickly.

They headed towards the I4 and Tampa.

Casey soon lost radio contact with Holly and Rebecca and hoped that they could keep track of Franco without him.

The long journey gave Casey time to reflect on everything that had happened in the last twenty-four hours.

With trepidation, Casey used the voice control and said, "call Agent Jones."

He knew that he was about to get a scolding from his mentor.

Agent Jones was at their headquarters in Washington and none the wiser of what had transpired.

Casey brought his mentor up to date and was at least thankful that his theory on the whereabouts of Franco was correct. Nonetheless, he was given a verbal roasting and warned about the consequences of losing Sam.

Nobody liked to get on the wrong side of Agent Jones. He was fair and helpful, but pity help those who tried to take advantage of his good nature. Which maybe explained the reason why Casey accidentally forgot to inform him about the need to steal a car.

Sam had managed to catch his breath. He had heard the front door open and instinctively tried the rear door of the SUV. To his surprise it was unlocked. He hid in the boot and lay motionless hoping that the occupants would stop nearby, and he could escape without being detected.

The boot of the SUV was dark, but surprisingly comfortable.

Sam could hear the unknown man and woman talking. Most of the time they spoke in a foreign language.

He was getting the hang of sending messages quickly and used his time to send a reassuring message to Rebecca, as well as, updates to Casey.

A telephone rang within the car. The phone was connected to the car's hands-free system which allowed Sam to hear the full conversation.

Sam received a message from Casey, "record the conversation and send for voice analysis and translation."

Arghh! Thought Sam; I should have thought to do that myself .

"The caller's name is Andre and he has referred to the male in the car as Ivan," typed Sam.

"We have a coded demand from the Spaniard to the General," Ivan told the caller in broken English. Andre was clearly not a native English speaker.

However, he was far better than Ivan or the female. Ivan was getting frustrated at finding the correct words in English and began speaking in a foreign language to Andre.

Immediately, Andre cut him short, "English! I cannot understand your Russian dialect."

"Halina, what is the coded demand?" Quizzed Andre, who was obviously fed up speaking with Ivan.

"I don't have the cipher to decode the numbers,"

she responded.

"Ok, make your way to the Yacht, the General is waiting for you," said Andre before hanging up.

Sam's head was racing,

"Russians,"

"General,"

"Coded Demands,"

"*WOW*," he thought as he quickly typed up a message to Casey.

"We need a plan! We need to get the coded message," he typed.

Casey relayed the information to Agent Jones who was on his way by helicopter to Orlando.

Sam took a few minutes to compose himself. The car shook and his thoughts were interrupted by the flashing message.

"Incoming Message from Casey." Before even reading the message, Sam knew what it was going to say. The road surface had changed, and they were now travelling very slowly.

Sam took a gulp then read Casey's message.

"Beware! We're entering a Marina car park and it's a dead end."

Sam had learned to control his emotions but nothing really prepares you for that moment just before all hell breaks out. This was like the calm before a storm.

Casey gave the SUV enough space so that he wouldn't be seen in their rear view mirror but he wanted to be close enough to help Sam if he was discovered.

Halina and Ivan reminded him of characters from his favourite fighting game; Mortal Combat. Two super fit, scary looking dudes that you wouldn't like to meet in a dark alleyway, but that wouldn't stop Casey from protecting his young friend.

The car came to a stop and Sam held his breath as he heard Halina and Ivan get out of the car.

He positioned himself with his back against the rear seats and legs bent so that he could kick out with force at anyone who opened the boot door. He knew that he would have the element of surprise and was ready to flee rather than fight.

The alarm on the car was activated and Sam could feel his chest deflate as he let out a sigh of relief.

Sam began typing a message to Casey. Typing

with your eyes took time but Sam didn't want to risk being discovered even though he wished he could just use voice control.

Casey parked his car and took a position to watch Halina and Ivan leave the SUV and walk towards a private Jetty within the Marina.

He watched as they boarded a small speedboat and sailed off out of the man-made cove.

"Sam, Sam, are you okay in there?"

Sam was delighted to hear Casey's voice.

"Are they away?" Replied Sam.

"Yes, I'm watching them sail out on a boat towards a large Yacht which, is moored about half a mile out at sea."

"Give me a minute and I'll find the frequency for the car lock."

A couple of minutes later, the car alarm deactivated and a smiling Casey opened the rear door.

"Oh, am I glad to see you?" Said Sam as he clambered out of the car.

"You did really well Sam. You've blown this case wide open," replied a jubilant Casey.

"Where did they go?" Quizzed Sam.

Casey pointed out to the sea. It wasn't hard to miss the huge luxury Yacht which was moored out at sea.

"That's a Billionaire's Yacht!" Said Sam in amazement.

"Where are we?" Asked Sam, as he gazed at the beautiful White sands and crystal clear Blue Sea.

"We're in St Pete's," said Casey as he started using a small monocular to survey the boat in better detail.

"Three upper decks and probably two lower decks. Helicopter landing pad and enough room for two speedboats at the back. Two armed guards on the middle deck," he gave a running commentary as he carefully analysed it.

"It's going to be quite difficult to get onboard without being noticed."

Nothing surprised Sam now, and he just smiled at Casey.

"Take the monocular and keep an eye on the movements on the boat," said Casey as he handed Sam the monocular.

"Where are you going?" Said a surprised Sam.

"We have a safe house hotel nearby. I'll go and get some supplies and then try to get onboard that Yacht," replied Casey, as he headed towards his car.

"Shouldn't we go back and help the girls?" Sam shouted to Casey as he was getting into the car.

He never replied and Sam was left to keep an eye on the Yacht.

Casey set the Sat Nav on his phone and followed the beachfront road to the opposite side of the city. The amazing clear blue sea of the Gulf of Mexico to his left and the Wooden villas and apartment buildings to his right.

He wasn't surprised with the presence of Russians in St Petersburg, as it was named after the Russian City of the same name and attracted many wealthy Russians. Rumours persisted for years that the Russian Mafia controlled all the bars and casinos in the area.

The Detroit Hotel was the first hotel in the area and had changed quite a bit since it was first built. The Red stone brick was a throw back to that era and quite different to how the city looked now.

Casey entered the main foyer and approached

the reception desk. The middle aged lady smiled and asked Casey if he had a reservation.

"The stars glisten like diamonds in St Pete's," he replied in a hushed voice.

Casey always felt uneasy when he had to use a secret pass phrase with someone that he'd never met before. Each area has its own secret passphrase to use. Casey had informed Headquarters that he was en-route to the hotel and was given a secret passphrase to use with the resident SQA Sleeper Agent.

SQA used the cover of hotels and resorts around the world to train children. They also used them as safe houses, places of refuge or supply drops for active Agents.

"Welcome Agent Lee. What can I get for you?" Asked the receptionist.

Casey found everything he needed and even managed to get a set of false number plates which he stuck on top of the stolen cars real number plates.

Within the hour, he was back with Sam.

Sam was amused to see Casey get out of the car wearing a wet suit.

Casey gathered his oxygen tank and equipment

from the boot of the car.

Darkness was falling and Casey was ready and keen to get over to the Yacht as soon as possible. He wanted to find the coded message and discover who they were delivering the message to. Was this the General that Sam had heard them discussing earlier?

"Where's my Wet Suit?" Asked Sam.

"You're not trained in diving, and besides Agent Jones would have my head on a plate if I let anything happen to you," said Casey.

"I need you to watch from here and give me commentary on where the guards are on the Yacht"

Sam nodded in agreement.

"What's that?" Asked Sam, pointing at a bright Yellow coloured machine.

"That's a Dive Scooter," replied Casey.

"Oh!" Said Sam, as he went to examine it more closely.

"It's a powerful underwater propeller that will pull me through the water quickly," said Casey, as he moved it away from Sam's inquisitive fingers.

"Now we wait till it's dark enough not to be seen. The lights on the Yacht will make it easier for you to see who is on board and which rooms are occupied."

Luckily, there was quite a bit of cloud cover and only a quarter moon.

"I'd better check-in with Holly. I tried calling her earlier but they were busy with Franco."

"I tried Rebecca earlier too, but she didn't answer," replied Sam.

Sam watched as Casey talked with Holly on the phone. Holly apparently wasn't impressed that Casey and Sam had left them in the lurch with Franco and Brakker.

"Oooffttt! She can be Nippy at times," remarked Casey in a hushed voice, as he held the phone away from his ears.

Sam could hear what Casey meant from Holly's scolding tone.

Casey held the mouthpiece of the phone to his mouth but the earpiece well away from him and shouted to Holly, "won't be long, see you soon," before hanging up.

"They have it in hand; Franco is having his dinner."

Sam was surprised that Casey didn't want to get

straight back up and watch Franco.

They sat watching the movements of the people on the Yacht and counted six people in total onboard.

Two guards appeared to be taking it in turns to stand on the middle deck and Halina and Ivan were seated at the rear of the boat alongside an older man. Every now and then a maid dressed in Black and White had brought them all drinks and food.

Darkness was falling and the occupants of the Yacht eventually all retired inside. The cabin lights onboard the Yacht made it standout on the dark sea like a bright star on a clear night.

"Right, I'm off. Wish me luck," said Casey as he got up and walked off towards the jetty.

He stopped and turned to Sam.

"If there's any trouble, don't try to come and help me. Contact Agent Jones and he will know what to do."

"Okay," replied Sam.

Sam could feel his stomach churning and couldn't imagine how Casey must be feeling.

He watched Casey walk to the end of the Jetty and slip gently into the dark water. Within seconds he was gone; swallowed by the vast sea.

Sam put the monocular to his eye and watched the Yacht intently. His eye started watering and he could feel the pain around his eyebrow as he'd squashed the monocular too close to his eye.

"Sam. Come in Sam," came the sound of Casey through Sam's earpiece.

"Go ahead Casey," replied Sam.

"That's me at the rear of the Yacht. The Dive Scooter is secured and ready for a quick getaway."

"Roger," said Sam.

"Give me good clear commentary on the movements of the guards and of any danger. This is the last I'll talk to you but rest assured I will be able to hear you."

"Understood. Good luck," replied Sam as he watched the back of the Yacht.

Sam watched as Casey appeared at the back of the Yacht. His dark Wet Suit blended into the night sky.

Casey could hear the muffled voices nearby and could see Halina and Ivan standing inside within the main living area of the Yacht. There were glass windows the whole way around the living area, but Casey was banking on his deduction that they would not be able to see out into the darkness.

The glasses and plates were still lying outside in the area where they had all been seated half an hour ago.

Casey searched the table and seats, but couldn't find anything with code written on it. He took his Identification Kit from his utility belt and started using clear ID tape to take a fingerprint from each glass.

After each lift, he waited for a few seconds and watched the occupants of the Yacht to make sure that they weren't coming outside.

He finished the last glass and placed each piece of tape in turn over the screen on his phone. The scanner activated immediately to send the fingerprints straight to headquarters. He was in the middle of sending the third image to HQ when his eye was drawn to a small piece of paper in a nearby waste bin.

Carefully he scrambled over and was delighted to see that it contained a series of twenty numbers.

Casey recognised the code's origin straight away.

"Sam, I need you to note these numbers,"

whispered Casey.

"Go ahead," replied Sam.

Sam put the monocular down and picked up the notepad and pen that Casey had left him.

"5344 1525 5414 1454 3415"

"Got it," said Sam when Casey had stopped talking.

Sam picked up the monocular and started to scan for the guard on the Yacht.

"Watch out Casey," Sam screamed.

But it was too late.

The guard had heard Casey repeating the numbers to Sam and had come over to investigate.

He couldn't see him initially and was right above him before he saw that it was a boy lying on the deck behind the seats.

'THUMP' the guards boot came crashing into Casey's ribs.

Casey hadn't heard the guard approach as he'd been too intent on making sure that he didn't get the number combination wrong.

Now he was in trouble. The guard was armed with an automatic rifle and he knew that the last place you wanted to be in a fight was on the ground and defenceless.

The guard managed to get several more kicks in at Casey's head and ribs before he managed to regain his composure.

Casey couldn't understand what the guard was shouting but he could hear the commotion coming from the living area and knew that within moments, there would be several more people on top of him.

The guard swung his boot again at Casey but this time Casey grabbed it and twisted it at the same time. His martial arts training had taught him to use your opponents power and strength against them.

He pushed the guards boot upwards and the momentum took the guard by surprise.

With a huge CRASH, the guard ended up falling down beside Casey.

Like a scalded cat, Casey was on his feet.

Something nipped the side of his face.

Casey didn't even look backwards, he knew what to do. With one leap he was airborne and diving into the dark water.

Sam stood frozen to the spot on the mainland

with tears welling in his eyes.

He had seen the guard approach Casey's position and was too late to warn him. He watched as the big thug had rained kick after kick at his friend and the relief of seeing the guard fall and Casey getting back on his feet was extinguished when he saw the other guard take aim and shoot. Casey's dark silhouette disappeared over the side of the Yacht and into the murky water below.

Sam wiped away the tears and put the monocular back to his eye. The two guards, Halina, and Ivan were all armed with rifles or handguns and shooting into the sea below.

Had they seen something? Or were they just trying to make sure that they had killed the intruder? Sam thought.

The guards switched on powerful searchlights around the Yacht, and Sam decided to retreat a little. He gathered his equipment, and headed for the car.

He sat in the car with tears still rolling down his cheeks. *What now? What do I tell Agent Jones?* He thought.

The car door opened, and Sam flinched, fully

expecting to see Ivan or Halina standing towering over him.

"Slide over. I'm the team driver," said a very wet and bloodied Casey.

"How? What? How on earth!" Sam was stuck for the right words and the shock on his face was clearly obvious.

"I think the bullet grazed the side of my head, and another nicked my cheek," said a relieved Casey.

"I thought you were dead" replied Sam as he searched through their bags for the first aid kit.

"I'm fine, it's just a scratch. Let's get out of here," said Casey as he started the car again.

AGENT
AGENT

CHAPTER FIVE

CODES AND CIPHERS

The girls had been lying sunbathing by the poolside. The bar attendant had dropped off their orders for ice cold smoothies and fruit juices.

"Casey's crazy idea that Franco could be here has its benefits," Holly told Rebecca.

"I love a chance to top up my tan," chuckled Rebecca.

Both of them had been enjoying relaxing in the sun and after a hectic night of tracking Brakker, could easily have dosed off into a sound sleep.

Suddenly their radios crackled into life at the same time, and both shot up from their sun loungers with the precision of a pair of Olympic Rhythmic Gymnasts.

They heard Casey talking to Sam, "Sam, can

you take the tracker off Brakker's vehicle and put it on the Porsche?"

"Something must be happening. Quickly get ready," Holly snapped to Rebecca.

Both girls were ready in a flash and Holly grabbed their towels to put in the dirty laundry bin at the side of the pool.

Her thoughts were on what was happening with Casey and Sam. The last thing she expected was for her Face Recon to burst into life.

She hadn't even noticed the man walking towards the gate beside the dirty linen bin. Luckily, the Face Recon never sleeps and never fails.

"Alert! Alert!" Came the warning texts.

For a moment, she was disorientated by the surprise messages.

Holy Shmoly! She thought as she turned away from the man walking beside her.

She let him walk a slight distance ahead and then radioed to Casey.

"Casey, come in. Can you hear me?" She didn't get a reply.

"I think we've found him," she said with total

glee in her voice.

To her shock, Casey still didn't reply.

Face Recon had confirmed. The man walking 20 yards ahead of her was FRANCO RODRIGUEZ.

The last time that she had been this close to him was when he had knocked Casey out in the vault and instead of chasing him, she had stayed to tend to Casey.

Here she was right next to "The Dark Cat" - the name given to Franco. She didn't know if it was because of his ethnicity, his dark complexion or because of his incredible cat burglar skills.

Maybe all three, she thought.

"His nine lives are about to run out today," she said with gritted determination.

Rebecca had heard Holly's transmission and had stopped in her tracks next to a line of shops at the entrance to the pool deck.

She remembered her training and took up a position to look in the shop windows and use the reflective surface to watch Franco's movements without drawing attention to herself.

Franco walked right behind her and entered a small store at the end of the building. Holly came walking briskly around the corner and nearly ran straight into Rebecca.

Both agreed to take up separate positions at either end of the building to cover the entrance to the store and be able to follow him covertly when he left again. They also agreed to monitor the radio to see what was happening with the boys.

Franco was in the shop for over half an hour, and during that time, the radio had went silent; the boys were gone.

Holly was hopping mad at Casey.

He'd dragged them all out to find Franco, and here they were with him in their sights, and he hadn't even been in contact for an update.

Not even an explanation as to who they were away following or why he thought that they were important to the mission, she mused. Every time she thought about it, she got angrier and angrier with him.

"Standby, Standby, Standby," repeated Rebecca.

She liked being able to commentate on the movements of a target.

"That's Franco out of the shop and turning left. Holly, he will be with you in a few moments."

Holly then cut in "Holly confirms eyeball. He's walking towards the Reception Centre."

Rebecca asked for permission to speak.

"Rebecca permission."

In training, surveillance operatives are taught that the person who has eyeball (sights) on the Target is in charge, and nobody should talk over them. If you wanted to talk, then you had to wait for the right time and then ask for permission to speak.

"Go ahead Rebecca," said Holly.

"If he enters the Reception Area, I will get in a position to follow him in," responded Rebecca, proud that she was thinking ahead.

"Roger that Rebecca," said Holly whilst continuing to give a running commentary on his direction and speed.

Franco seemed unconcerned about his surroundings. He'd obviously been here that long since the Robbery that he thought he was safe.

Sure enough, Franco headed through the automatic doors at the Reception Building.

“That’s him into the Reception Building. Over to you Rebecca,” said Holly signing off.

Rebecca knew that every surveillance operative has to put their faith and trust into the ability of their colleagues to take over and do their best to maintain the observations on the target. She knew that losing the target for seconds is long enough to miss the most important part of the intelligence gathering operation and didn’t mind admitting to herself that she was more than a little nervous, with so much at stake.

With this in mind she had chosen to take a route parallel to the buildings and run as fast as she could to get ahead of Franco.

She had just made it into the building and was grabbing a seat at the far side when she heard Holly handing over the commentary to her.

Peaking above a magazine that she’s lifted, she watched as Franco strutted into the nice air conditioned building.

It was the first chance that she had to study Franco in any detail.

“He’s a very handsome man,” she blurted out.

"Yes, he is! But what's he doing?" Snapped Holly.

"Oops, sorry. I didn't realise that I'd said that out loud," said Rebecca sheepishly.

Rebecca started her commentary.

"He's walking over to the Concierge."

She suddenly realised that her magazine was upside down. In her haste to get seated, she hadn't realised what magazine she had lifted or which way up it should be.

She turned her gaze back to Franco and continued her commentary.

"The target is giving the concierge a postcard."

"The man behind the desk has accepted the postcard from him, and the target is now walking back towards the same door that he entered from."

"Do you have him?" She asked Holly.

Holly picked up the commentary and both girls then followed him back to an apartment building, which was next to the pool deck where they'd first seen him.

Holly was deep in thought. She was the opposite from Casey, and that's probably why they made a great partnership. She was more methodical and liked to think through her plans and then analyse her decisions to see if she had missed something.

"What are you thinking?" Asked Rebecca.

"I need you to go back and speak with the concierge and find out what you can about the postcard!" Replied Holly.

"No problem" I'll be back shortly," said Rebecca as she started retracing her steps back to the Reception Building.

She decided to have a look in the store that Franco had been in earlier.

There was no name above the door and the shop front only had one window but it had a reflective screen attached to the glass, and no one could see into the store.

Rebecca opened the door and peeked her head inside. The smell of incense was the first thing that she noticed. The store was not what she was expecting.

"Come in my darling," came a voice from the back of the store.

An old woman appeared from behind a curtain. She was dressed in a colourful long dress and was wearing a headscarf that was held in place with a band of gold jewels, which stretched around her head and across her forehead.

Rebecca could feel herself backing up out of the door and was thinking of the right excuse to make in order to leave quickly.

"Sorry, I was looking for my brother," she said hastily.

"Hope you find him, my darling. Come back and see me soon Rebecca."

As Rebecca closed the door behind her, she stopped dead and felt a shiver running down her spine.

"She knew my name!" She whispered to herself.

Did I hear the old woman correctly? How does she know me?

She headed off to find the concierge and could still feel the shivers down her back.

"How freaky!" She whispered as she gave herself a shake.

Rebecca approached the same man behind the desk at the concierge.

"Good afternoon sir," she greeted the man.

"How can I help you young lady?" Replied the man.

"My father handed in a postcard to you earlier and didn't give me a chance to sign it. Could I see it and add my signature?" Rebecca added with an air of confidence in her voice and demeanour.

To her relief, the concierge took her word without asking any awkward questions.

"Of course, I still have it here."

The man went over to a counter and retrieved the postcard.

"Oh, do you have a pen?" Questioned Rebecca.

"Wait a moment and I'll get you one," said the man as he walked off to find a pen.

Rebecca had her phone ready and quickly took a photograph of the postcard. She then studied it and read over the message.

"Mmm… That's a strange message to leave."

Hello Kriss

Our exchange holiday to Orlando has been great. You
will be amazed at all the FUN Team Activities when you visit.
In the pool today we built a raft and raced around Pirate Island. The
Food Court has great variety for all the family and is our favorite place.
This evening we are going to the Outlets shopping.

Franco

To anyone else, the message would be innocent enough but Rebecca knew that Franco wasn't on an exchange holiday and that he'd certainly hadn't been building a raft and racing it around Pirate Island.

The concierge interrupted her thought.

"Here you are," he said as he handed Rebecca a pen.

Rebecca took the pen and put the initials "FR" in the bottom right hand corner.

She gave the postcard back to the man.

"Have I still to give Mr. Brakker this first thing tomorrow morning?" He asked as Rebecca was walking away.

"Er, Yes please," she replied. Her mind was still racing at what the point of the message was to Kriss.

She made her way quickly back to see Holly. Holly took one look at the picture of the postcard and took out her cell phone.

"Watch this!" She told Rebecca.

Holly then held her phone over the top of Rebecca's.

Rebecca strained her neck to see the screen of Holly's phone correctly. Rebecca saw that Holly had selected her *Spy Cam* mode and was looking at the postcard picture on her phone.

"WOW! How did you do that?" Rebecca exclaimed, as the letters on the postcard started falling off the page to reveal a secret message.

"Hello Kriss,
Our exchange
will be.
In the
Food Court
This evening
Franco."

"It's Crypto Anaylsis software I developed for the Agency. It helps crack Null codes" replied Holly.

"O.M.G. we've got him," exclaimed Rebecca.

Holly was almost jumping with excitement too.

"The concierge told me that he was to give this postcard to Brakker tomorrow morning, which means that the exchange is tomorrow in the Food Court," blurted Rebecca.

To her shock, Holly grabbed her arm and pulled her down.

"Ouch! What was that for," she said rubbing her arm.

"Franco!" Whispered Holly.

Holly had caught a glimpse of Franco leaving his apartment and was waiting on him appearing at the bottom of the stairwell.

They followed Franco to a nearby restaurant and watched as he was seated at his table and ready to order.

Darkness was falling and Holly knew that she would only get one chance to do what she had planned. She took hold of Rebecca's arms and stood facing her.

"I need to try and get into Franco's apartment," she told Rebecca.

"Are you crazy?" Whispered a shocked Rebecca.

"I need you to watch Franco and give me as much warning as possible when he is finished his dinner and about to leave the restaurant."

"Okay," responded Rebecca. "But I still think your crazy. How are you going to get in?"

"His apartment is on the first floor and the rear of the building has a small balcony that leads to a set of patio doors. It overlooks a quiet lake which is perfect for me to try to get in and out without being noticed," said a confident Holly.

Rebecca took up a position from across the street where she could see Franco sitting and also see the front doors of the restaurant. Holly headed off to find a way into Franco's apartment.

Holly was an excellent ACRO Gymnast and used to climbing tough structures. She scaled the building with ease and crouched down beside the patio door.

En-route she picked up two large pin badges from the store near to the Pool Deck and was now using the pins on the badges to pick the lock.

Holly was skilled in picking locks and within minutes, she had the door open.

She slipped quietly into the dark apartment and placed her sunglasses on. Carefully, she switched them to infrared mode and immediately an image of the room lit up in green. She systematically started searching each room.

Franco is one tidy thief, she thought as she searched through bundles of neatly folded t-shirts. His designer shirts were ironed and hung up with a pair of immaculately polished shoes positioned beneath each shirt.

The search was taking longer than she had hoped and she hadn't found any trace of the Hope Diamond.

The silence within the room was suddenly shattered with Music,

"He was a boy.
She was a girl
Can I make it any more obvious?"

Arghh, she thought as she scrambled to stop her cell phone ringing. Rookie mistake not putting your phone on silent when breaking into an apartment.

"Casey! What is it?"

"Where are you?"

"Get back here NOW!" Holly fired off a volley of pent up aggression at Casey.

"Franco, is having dinner and poor Rebecca has been left to watch him," said Holly, without giving

Casey any time to reply.

"Won't be long, see you soon," replied Casey cooly before hanging up.

"Arghh! That boy," she said as she stomped her foot on the ground with anger.

"He hung up on me. He actually hung up on me!" She repeated feeling indignant that Casey had hung up on her.

She then realised that her stomp on the floor had moved a floor board. Looking down, she could see that the wooden panel had shifted slightly.

She bent down, wedged the badge pin under the panel, and tried to pull it up. The pin badge broke with the force. Holly put her nails under the lip of the panel and started to pull gently. At last, the panel began to move. She lifted it aside and was delighted to see that a small bag had been secreted underneath.

Carefully she lifted it out and was making a mental note of how it had been placed in the hole, so that she could return it exactly as she had found it.

"Please be here, please be here," she repeated to herself as she started to open the bag.

The leather bag was quite heavy and contained

several small but hard objects.

Her suspense was interrupted as her Comms broke into life.

"Come in Holly, Come in Holly," said the voice on the radio.

"Go ahead Rebecca." replied Holly.

"Franco has left the restaurant and is walking quickly back towards you," said Rebecca with a tone of fear in her voice.

"Give me a running commentary, I need to do one more thing," said Holly with her heart suddenly pounding harder.

Holly quickly opened up the bag and took the contents out. To her disappointment, there was no sign of the Hope Diamond.

Inside the bag was a Washington travel guide book, a Passport in a different name, a UV torch, a compass, a USB stick, a Washington map, a Floor Plan of the Museum with times and notes written on it, and a strange heavy object with five reels of letters.

"Got you, Franco," she murmured under her breath as she placed the contents out.

"Holly! Get out NOW!" Came the cries from Rebecca.

Holly quickly photographed the contents and was just placing them back in the bag when she heard the key being put in the front door.

Panic began to take over Holly. She froze and knew that within seconds she was about to come face to face with Franco.

Rebecca had watched helplessly as Franco walked up the stairs and approached his front door.

"Excuse me sir," she shouted.

Franco turned around just as he opened his door.

"I've forgotten to put my contact lenses in and I've dropped my key. Could you help me find it?" She asked, with complete innocence.

Rebecca knew that normally the last thing that you want to do as a surveillance operative is engage in conversation with the primary target.

Emergency situations called for drastic and unorthodox actions.

To her relief, Franco closed the door over and started walking down the stairway. Rebecca quickly threw her apartment key on the grass further down the pathway.

"Where do you think you were when you dropped it?" Inquired Franco as they began looking for the key.

Holly let out a sigh of relief. She heard Rebecca's shout and had never been so glad to see a door close in all her life.

She quickly put everything back as she had found it and made her way back out of the apartment. Taking care to lock the patio door again so that she had left no trace of her presence.

She scaled back down the wall of the building and whispered a message to Rebecca.

"Rebecca, that's me out safely. Well done and thanks."

At that moment, Franco found the lost key.

"Here you are," he said as he handed Rebecca the key.

"Thank you very much Sir," she said as she accepted the key and then turned to walk off towards the Pool Deck.

CHAPTER SIX

THE CURSE

Agent Jones arrived at the resort an hour or so later, with several members of the FBI. Casey and Sam had come back just beforehand and as instructed, had returned the car to the same position that he had found it. On the journey back to Orlando, Casey had confessed about taking the car.

Agent Jones gave Casey an envelope with cash to leave in the car so that the owner was compensated for the loss of the car and any damage that Casey had made.

They all gathered together to update Agent Jones on the day's events. Casey and Sam began their debrief first. The girls were shocked to hear that someone had shot at Casey.

"You could have been killed," said an emotional Holly.

"Need to be much quicker than that to kill me," replied Casey as he gave her a quick hug.

Holly and Rebecca then told everyone about what had happened at the resort.

"Sound like you've all had an eventful day?" Said Agent Jones when they'd all finished.

"I need you all to get some sleep. Tomorrow is going to be a big day and I need you refreshed." He added.

"Can't we just arrest them now?" Asked Sam.

"Not yet! We still don't know where the Diamond is," said Agent Jones.

"The FBI have identified an address in Washington from the name on the false Passport that you found in Franco's apartment Holly. They're about to search it and I'll give you an update in the morning," said Agent Jones before handing them keys to a nearby villa.

The four of them headed off accompanied by an FBI Agent to find the villa. To Sam's surprise in the villa was a suitcase for each of them with new clothes and toiletries.

"He really does think of everything" marvelled Sam as he looked for a fresh t-shirt.

"That's why he's the best of the best" replied Casey.

The next morning, they all met up at the restaurant to have breakfast. Agent Jones was standing waiting on them.

"Agents, I'd like you to meet Glen. Glen was previously an Agency Trainer that I worked with many years ago and he is now the General Manager of this resort. We can trust him and if you need anything at all while we are on the resort, please don't hesitate to speak with him," said Agent Jones.

Agent Jones produced a fax copy of a document, which he'd received from the FBI in Washington. He beckoned them all to gather round it.

"The FBI found this partially completed Polybius Cipher in Franco's apartment."

	1	2	3	4	5
1		**B**	**Y**	**F**	**Q**
2	**X**	**K**	**U**	**A**	**S**
3	**G**	**H**	**P**	**W**	**T**
4		**C**	**O**	**E**	**I**
5	**N**		**Z**	**V**	**R**

"Now for the bad news," continued Agent Jones.

"The FBI can't be sure that Franco is still within his apartment. The night shift heard someone leave around 5.30 am and didn't check it out as the motion sensor they had put on his door didn't activate. The morning shift then went to test the sensor and found that it had been knocked off the door. Possibly by an inquisitive Gecko, they're everywhere down here," said Agent Jones.

"What!" Exclaimed Casey.

"How could that happen? Who…"

Before Casey could finish, all of their wristbands began to vibrate at the same time.

Simultaneously, Agent Jones' cell phone rang.

"Brakker is fleeing! Quickly get to my car

outside," cried Agent Jones as he grabbed his car keys from the table.

As they ran, Agent Jones barked out orders,

"Casey, Sam, you come with me. Holly, you take Rebecca and meet with the strike team for Franco's apartment."

"Let's get them," shouted Casey gleefully, as he jumped into the front seat of the car.

Sam was pumped with excitement and could feel the adrenaline flowing through his body. *This was it*, he thought.

As he slid into the car he took a moment to marvel at the beautiful interior of the Black Mustang GT convertible. Agent Jones sure has good taste, he mused.

This was Sam's favourite car whenever he drove the car simulator games.

Agent Jones put the manual gear in first and took off with the force of a rocket heading for space.

Sam was thrown back with the G-Force of the car taking off and shouted out with delight, "nobody is getting away from us in this."

The FBI had been watching Brakker's villa and

had watched as he had hurriedly shuttled back and forth from the villa to the car with his belongings. It was obvious to them that he was panicking and planning to leave.

The car boot and driver's door were still open when Agent Jones drove round the corner. Just as he screeched to a halt outside, Brakker came to the door.

He took one look at the car and dropped what he was carrying and took off back into the house. Casey sprung from his seat like a mountain lion surprising its prey. He was off and after him before Sam had managed to scramble out of the car.

"Sam, you go around the side of the house and cover the back door, and I'll drive around to the street behind in case he makes it that far," shouted Agent Jones as he slipped the gears into reverse and wheel-spun the car backwards.

Casey raced through the house checking every room as he ran. He'd lost sight of Brakker when he went into the house.

Sam ran to the back door and was just about to pull the handle when the door suddenly came flying open. The door smacked him square in the face and knocked him flat on his back.

"Casey!" Cried Sam as he fell.

Brakker came crashing through the door and ran towards the back fence.

Seconds later, Casey came flying through the door and nearly smacked Sam again with the door just as he was getting up.

Casey was in time to see Brakker leap over the fence at the rear and into the adjoining garden.
Sam was on his feet in a flash and took off after Casey and Brakker. His training had made him feel much fitter and he jumped the fence with ease.

Brakker ran out of sight around the side of the villa towards the street. Casey came charging around after him and was surprised to see Brakker lying sprawled across the grass.

Agent Jones had sped around to the street behind and positioned himself at the front of the villa directly adjacent to Brakker's villa. Sure enough, Brakker had come sprinting around the side of the building and straight into an outstretched arm from Agent Jones.

"An old fashioned clothes line take down!" Laughed Agent Jones, as Sam came racing around behind Casey.

Two FBI Agents arrived on the scene and placed Brakker in handcuffs.

"Take him to the local Sheriff's office and we'll be along shortly," instructed Agent Jones before turning to the boys.

"Casey take Sam and have a look in Brakker's car and villa. Point out anything evidential to the FBI Agents."

"I'll go and meet up with the girls at Franco's apartment," he said in a hushed voice so that Brakker could not hear him.

Holly and Rebecca had run all the way over to the FBI surveillance van, which was parked near to Franco's apartment. The van was very large and had a local utility company's signage on the side and rear. The front cab of the vehicle was empty as the driver had left the vehicle parked giving it the impression of it being unattended. Two operatives were locked within the rear of the van before it was deployed.

Rebecca had only seen similar vans in movies.

Wow, she thought as one of the men opened the rear doors for her to climb in.

The FBI operatives were sitting in comfy chairs that swivelled so that they could use the TV and radio equipment positioned on small benches that ran along both sides of the interior walls.

The radio crackled, and they could all hear the radio communications between Agent Jones and the boys as they chased Brakker.

"Yippee! Awesome work guys," squealed Holly when she heard that they'd caught him.

"Hopefully, Franco is still here!" She said in a cheerful voice to Rebecca as she gave her a high five for the news that the boys had caught Brakker.

The radio crackled again, "SWAT One in position."

"Roger, SWAT One, wait for further instructions," said the FBI Agent at the rear of the van.

"SWAT Two in position."

"Roger, SWAT Two, wait for further instructions," instructed the same agent.

Holly gave Rebecca a knowing glance, this was the climax of all their hard work. The exciting part, which made it all real. At times agents in the field can become detached from what is happening and why they are following a suspect. They monitor a suspect and feedback intelligence and occasional evidence that they have collected but very rarely do they get involved in the actual arrests.

The doors at the rear of the van opened again. A grinning Agent Jones stepped into the crowded van.

"Both teams are in position Sir," said the Agent at the rear of the van.

"Tell them to move in," instructed Agent Jones.

"Girls, you both stay here. I don't want to blow your cover if we don't need to," said Agent Jones as he moved closer to watch the monitor.

The FBI had parked a car outside Franco's apartment. The car had a hidden pan and tilted 360-degree camera positioned on the parcel shelf so that they could remotely monitor everything around Franco's apartment.

"Does the car have additional cameras?" Inquired Agent Jones.

"Yes Sir," said one of the FBI Agents.

"Can you let me see them on the other monitors

please?" Asked Agent Jones.

The additional monitors burst into life with views from the sides of the car showing the surrounding buildings and sidewalks.

Two unmarked vans could be seen entering the street. They drew up slowly at the front of the entrance to Franco's apartment, and a team of uniformed SWAT officers came swarming out of the side and rear doors. The first two officers were carrying a large black tubular device which was obviously hefty, as it had two handles and it took both of the men to carry the device.

Another two officers followed behind them carrying plastic shields.

The second van drew to a halt just beside them and another swarm of officers who were carrying firearms quickly disembarked from it in a military fashion.

The biggest monitor within the van then switched views from the car camera to the officer helmet cam.

Everyone watched as they could see an officer get ready to crash through the apartment door with the large Rammit device. The officer swung the device and the loud crash would have woken even the heaviest of sleepers.

The door flew open on the first hit and splinters of wood sprayed across the floor. as the door left its hinges behind and smacked against the ground. The officer stood aside as the rest quickly filed in the front door.

Every officer had a helmet cam and Agent Jones scanned each screen hoping to see someone find Franco.

"All clear."

"All clear."

"All clear."

Came the constant reply as each officer reported the results of searching each room.

Agent Jones broke the disappointing silence within the van as he opened the rear doors, "Arghh."

He paced back and forth a few times outside, his head racing before deciding on what to do next.

"Holly, you come with me and point out the concealment under the floor board. Rebecca, you stay here just now," instructed Agent Jones.

Holly joined Agent Jones, and both of them

made their way to the apartment.

She felt strange walking back into the same apartment that she'd been just a few hours earlier and nearly been discovered.

"Maybe it would have been better that he had discovered me in the apartment," she told Agent Jones as they looked in each room.

"Why is that?" Replied Agent Jones slightly bemused.

"Then we would have caught him," she replied.

"Your safety is more important," he reassured her.

Holly found the same floorboard and used a knife from the kitchen to pry it open again. The board was much harder to open this time; it had been replaced properly the last time it was opened.

"Hopefully, it was me that replaced it like this," she muttered as she tried to get it open.

"Looks as though he left in a hurry," said Agent Jones as he looked in the clothes closet.

"Some of his belongings are still here Sir," said a uniformed SWAT team member that had been searching the apartment.

"The bag is still here," shouted an excited Holly as she finally removed the floorboard.

Holly reached in and removed the bag.

"It's still heavy," commented Holly as she excitedly tried to unzip the bag.

"Oh, no!" She exclaimed, as she started placing all of the contents out across the floor.

"The Passport, USB stick, and object we identified as a Cryptex are missing."

Rebecca could hear her comments and was pleased that they had at least preserved some of the evidence.

A large crowd had started forming outside the apartment, and local Law Enforcement Officers had arrived and started putting up Police tape so that no one could contaminate the crime scene.

Rebecca then noticed something unusual.

The old woman from the store that Franco had visited was standing at the side of the police tape and watching everything that was going on.

How did she know my name? Thought a puzzled Rebecca.

"Everything seems to be tied up here for just

now," Rebecca told the FBI Agents as she made her way out of the van to go and speak with the old woman.

It was just a hunch, but Rebecca thought it best to leave no stone unturned in their quest to find Franco.

She was the last person to speak with Franco. She thought to herself, as she headed round to the apartment.

As Rebecca got there, more people were beginning to gather around the police tape. She scanned the faces but the old lady had vanished.

Rebecca decided to head round to the shop and see if she had gone that way.

"For an old woman, she sure walks fast if she came this way," she mumbled to herself as she strode quickly across the Pool Deck and towards the shop.

The door to the shop was unlocked and a bell tinkled as the door opened. Rebecca couldn't see anyone, but the same smell of incense filled the empty store. The store had a creepy feeling to it.

"Can I help you again my Dear?" Came a voice

from behind Rebecca. She nearly jumped out of her skin.

"Oh, sorry! I didn't mean to startle you," said the old woman, when she saw Rebecca jump.

Rebecca could feel the hairs on the back of her neck stand up. The old lady must have taken a different route back to the shop and Rebecca had got there first.

"Yes, yesterday, you knew my name when I came into the store?" She asked the old lady.

"Yes, my Dear. I am a fortune teller and my gift occasionally lets me see the future."

"Did you see me in the future?" Replied a slightly scared, somewhat intrigued Rebecca.

"Yes, your path is intertwined with the destiny of others that you are seeking."

The old lady took Rebecca's hand and stared deep into her eyes before continuing,

"Some are surrounded by darkness, my Dear. However, find strength in your sadness, you are destined for great things."

Rebecca could feel a coldness run all the way down her back. She gulped and tried to regain her composure.

"Do you remember a man coming to visit you half an hour before I came in yesterday?" Queried Rebecca.

"Do you mean Franco?" Replied the old woman.

"Yes!" Exclaimed an excited Rebecca.

"Have a seat and I'll be back in a moment," said the old lady as she showed Rebecca to a small table at the rear of the store.

As the old woman vanished into the back of the store, Rebecca took the opportunity to survey the store in more detail. The table was covered with a thick black tablecloth and the store itself was filled with strange looking ornaments, and paintings. The glass display case which had an old fashioned till on it, also housed different sizes of glass balls and packs of tarot cards on the shelves below.

A few moments later, the old lady returned carrying a large object which was hidden beneath a velvet cloth.

She placed the object in the middle of the table and then sat down opposite Rebecca.

The old lady had changed into her colourful

robes and Rebecca could now see that the headscarf was held on with a chain of gold coins and beads which were wrapped from her forehead to the back of her head.

She removed the velvet cloth to reveal a crystal ball which was held in place by a small brass three-pronged stand.

"My name is Madame Le Harve. For centuries, my ancestors have foretold the future. The gift has been passed down to each generation of girls within the family," she told Rebecca.

"What, Erm. What can you tell me about Franco?" Asked Rebecca, as she tried to clear her throat.

Madame Le Harve stared into her Crystal Ball,

"Franco is troubled! He is in possession of a treasure that he has sought for a long time. However, the treasure has a deadly CURSE placed upon anyone who possesses it."

Rebecca sat wide-eyed and amazed at what the old lady was telling her.

"Do you mean the Hope Diamond?" Asked Rebecca.

She continued, “over the centuries, many people who have claimed the treasure for their own have died an untimely death.”

Rebecca interrupted. “Is Franco dead?”

“Please don’t interrupt me my Dear,” said Madame Le Harve, as she appeared to be entering in and out of a trance while looking at the Crystal Ball.

“The Curse will only be broken when the treasure is returned to the rightful owner,” she added as she stopped looking at the ball.

She again looked Rebecca in the eye and informed her, “when Franco first came to see me, I warned him about the Curse and told him that I could see danger which would lead to the death of someone connected to the Diamond.”

“He came back yesterday to have his fortune told with the Tarot Cards. The first card I turned was the Angel of Death card. He didn’t want to continue after that.”

Rebecca let out a gasp of air. She had been unintentionally, holding her breath and was completely absorbed by what the old lady was telling her.

"Can you tell me where he went to?" Asked Rebecca trying not to look at the Crystal Ball as she spoke.

"No, my Dear. I'm afraid that I can't help you any further," she said placing the velvet cloth over the Crystal Ball.

Rebecca thanked the old lady and hurried off to find the others.

CHAPTER SEVEN

INTERROGATION

An hour or so later, Casey, Holly, Sam, and Rebecca were sitting in an Observation room watching Agent Jones interview Brakker within the adjoining interview suite.

The Observation room had a large one-way window, with microphones positioned in the interview suite allowed them to also hear everything that was being said.

Sam gazed around the room, he'd never been in a Police Station and had only seen a room like this on TV. The building was quite old and in need of repair. He wondered how many other people had stood in this very room watching someone being interviewed. His mind began to wander and he started thinking about the kind of crimes that the individual being interviewed might have committed. The thought of it sent a shudder down his spine, he tried to put it to the back of his mind and concentrate on what Agent Jones was saying to Brakker.

Agent Jones had been trying to get Brakker to talk, but he has refused to say anything at all.

"Don't worry, he is the best at getting someone to talk," said Casey as he tried to reassure everyone.

The experienced Agent was highly trained in interview and interrogation techniques. He knew that Brakker was scared to talk and more afraid of the consequences of talking than of going to jail.

He paced the room pondering his next move while Brakker sat at the small table in the middle.

Rodriguez doesn't pose him a threat?

So, could it be the mysterious Russians? He thought to himself as he looked at Brakker.

He sat back down and stared at Brakker and thought to himself, *Time for a gamble!*

"We know all about Ivan, Halina, and the General," he said slowly, but sternly.

Brakker's face started to Pale immediately as the blood drained away. He was apparently not expecting

Agent Jones to know anything about them.

Agent Jones knew that this was a turning point and moved quickly to ram home the consequences of Brakker not talking. He gambled that Brakker was unaware about Casey being caught on their Yacht.

"We are about to arrest them on the Yacht. One way or another, they are going to think that you talked to us anyway."

"This is your last chance. Tell us what you know and we will make the Judge aware that you co-operated. You may get years off your sentence."

Agent Jones' tactics worked.

Brakker began telling them how Ivan and Halina had approached him months beforehand in Amsterdam and had paid him to find 'The Dark Cat'. He knew how to contact Rodriguez through the criminal underworld however, he had never actually met him. Rodriguez always communicated in coded messages and was very careful not to show his face.

Ivan and Halina worked for someone that they called the 'General' but Brakker had never met him either. The Russians wanted Rodriguez for a special job but wouldn't tell him what it was until he confirmed that he had made contact.

"After I confirmed that contact had been made, they instructed me to make the offer to Franco of $1,000,000 to steal the Hope Diamond."

"How was he to be paid?" Questioned Agent Jones.

"That's the problem," replied Brakker.

Brakker hesitated and took a gulp of air, as if to give himself the final push over an invisible barrier of no return.

Agent Jones had learned that saying nothing was better than talking in these situations. He just nodded his head in encouragement.

Brakker continued. "Something went wrong at the museum and Rodriguez was nearly caught. The hacker that the Russians were using didn't account for something and the alarm was activated."

"Well, at least we know that he's telling the truth so far," said Casey as he listened intently.

"The first time that I knew something was wrong was when Franco called me after the heist. He was furious at the Russians and blamed them for nearly being caught" said Brakker as he continued his story.

"I thought he never called you?" Asked Agent Jones.

"He doesn't usually call. He said that the price was going up due to their incompetence and that he'd be in touch after the heat had died down."

"Where was he when he called you?" Quizzed Agent Jones.

"I don't know. That was the last I heard for weeks," replied Brakker.

"How did you know that he was in Florida?" asked Agent Jones.

"He called me again about a week ago from a new mobile number and said that he wanted to meet here." replied Brakker.

"The Russians weren't happy with him for going to ground with the diamond and had insisted on coming to Florida when I told them that he was here."

Rebecca sat watching the interrogation unfold and couldn't help but let her mind drift back to when she had been kidnapped and interrogated by Gail Torrez.

"Oblivion interview techniques are certainly different to ours," she whispered to Sam.

"Yeah, although the consequences are the same, I suppose!" replied Sam, fully aware that Brakkers' life was now in danger because of this confession.

"How much does Rodriguez want now for the Diamond?" Asked Agent Jones.

"I received a coded message demanding Ten million dollars," replied Brakker.

"And are the Russians willing to pay that amount?" Quizzed Agent Jones.

Brakker took a few seconds to respond, "Ivan and Halina visited me at my villa yesterday, I gave them the coded demand and they threatened to kill me!"

Agent Jones's mind was racing and trying to stay one-step ahead of Brakker, so that he asked the correct questions. Everything that Brakker had said so far tied in with what he knew however, he also knew that everyone always tried to hide certain facts when they were admitting their involvement in a crime.

"What made you try to flee today?" Asked Agent Jones.

"I received another message from Rodriguez this morning. He said that he had the Hope Diamond and her larger sister, and that he also had another buyer for them both."

"Oh, man!" Exclaimed Casey.

The cold realisation of what Brakker had just said hit them all like a bolt of lightning at the same time.

"Have we just lost Franco and the Diamond?" Asked Rebecca hoping that she was wrong.

Holly grabbed the bag of evidence that they had seized from Brakker's villa. She frantically searched for his cell phone. To her relief, it didn't have a password to access it.

She opened the messages and immediately saw that the last message was from CAT, which she knew must mean Franco.

"Casey, take note of this new number for Franco and request a cell site analysis so that we can find Franco." Holly read out Franco's new cell phone number.

She then continued, "Sam take note of this coded text message and we'll try to decode it."

Holly started repeating the numbers from the text message “54 - 23 42 45 44 - 23 34 33 44 - 11 54 42 25 34 15 11 - 42 15 11 - 23 44 55 - 14 42 55 13 44 55 - 52 54 52 53 44 55.”

Rebecca was using the partial completed cipher found in Franco’s apartment to work out the secret message.

“Holly, you can stop there. He’s telling the truth,” said a disappointed Rebecca.

They all looked at each other disappointed that they might have let Franco slip through their fingers again.

The door opening broke the silence. Agent Jones strode in and nobody had even noticed that he’d left the interview room.

“His story checks out,” said Casey as Agent Jones closed the door behind him.

Agent Jones turned and nodded in agreement. “I thought it would,” he added.

“Casey, this is your operation and I wanted to give you the final word on the next step. What I’m about to propose is very dangerous and something as an Agency, we don’t like to do!”

One by one, he looked them all in the eye before adding, "We need Brakker's help to catch Franco and the Russians. I propose, that we offer him immunity in return for helping us catch them."

"Do you mean, use him as a participating informant?" Asked Casey.

"Yes," replied Agent Jones.

This was a game changer. They all knew that the Agency frowned upon applications to use people who had been arrested as participating informants (P.I's as they were often known as). It meant that Brakker wouldn't be charged for his part in the heist and there was good chance that after the operation was finished he would have to be put in the FBI Witness Protection Scheme.

Bakker would need to change his name and relocate. It also meant that he would be looking over his shoulder for the rest of his life.

For the next ten minutes or so, the Agents all stood discussing the ramifications of their next step.

Agent Jones returned to the interview room and put their proposal to Brakker. He listened intently as Agent Jones explained what would be expected from him, the dangers involved and the rewards for helping.

Brakker had never been arrested for anything.

He was an experienced jeweller from Netherlands and had ventured into the lucrative world of daring Jewel Heists accidentally several years beforehand. Since then, he had acted as a middleman between the buyer for rare jewels and the thief who had stolen them. His commissions made him a lot of money and he gained a reputation as someone who could act discreetly for private collectors.

The thought of spending ten years or more in an American prison filled him with fear and with reluctance, he agreed to help.

"I must now seek official permission," said Agent Jones to Brakker, as he again left him in the room.

This time, Agent Jones did not enter the Observation room, but instead went to speak with someone at HQ.

Half an hour passed and Casey was pacing up and down the room with a million questions and scenarios rushing through his mind.

Can we trust him? Can Brakker pull it off and

convince Franco that the Russians have agreed to pay up? He thought, as he continued walking up and down the room.

After what seemed an eternity, the door to the Interview room opened again and Agent Jones entered along with Agent Evans.

"Mr. Brakker, I'm pleased to tell you that we have been given permission to use your services as a participating informant. Your status with us has now changed and you are no longer being detained. Do you understand what that means?"

Agent Jones paused, as he waited for a sign of acknowledgement from Brakker.

"I do," he replied nodding his head.

Agent Jones continued, "you must sign this document, agreeing that you will help us with our enquiries. If at any time you do not do as we request, then we reserve the right to cancel this agreement and you will be re-arrested on the original charges. Do you understand?"

"Yes, I do," replied Brakker who was still looking pale in the face and was clearly worried about what the future held for him.

Agent Evans then gave Brakker the document and instructed him to take his time to read it's contents before he signed it.

Brakker read it over, signed it, and returned it to Agent Jones.

"Agent Evans will wait with you here," he informed Brakker as he made his way to leave the room.

Agent Jones then summoned Casey, Holly, Sam, and Rebecca to a room further within the Sheriff Department's building.

Over the next hour, they hatched a dangerous plan.

"Let's go over it one last time, to make sure everyone is clear on their responsibilities..." said Agent Jones.

"Casey and Holly, your mission is to get onto the Yacht without being discovered and give us eyes and ears on what is going on aboard that Yacht. We also need to know how many people are onboard."

"Sam and Rebecca, you're staying with me and we will take Brakker to meet with Franco. Our mission is to arrest Franco and get the diamond back."

Sam and Rebecca nodded their heads in agreement.

Agent Jones's plan was to have Brakker send a message to Franco that the client had agreed to pay the ten million dollars. Franco would then send his bank account details for the wire transfer and instructions on the location of the exchange.

Brakker also had to contact the Russians and get them to agree to pay the money. Once they had paid the money, he would give them the location for an exchange of the diamond and lure them into a trap.

This would entail two exchanges for Brakker; one with Franco and another with the Russians.

The thief and buyer for any stolen gems would never normally meet. That was always the job for the middleman. If Agent Jones's dangerous plan was to succeed, then he knew that it all hinged on Brakker convincing both parties that all was well.

"Are we all clear on our responsibilities?" Agent Jones asked everyone in the room.

"Yes sir," came the unanimous reply from Casey, Holly, Sam, and Rebecca.

Agent Jones pulled Casey aside as he was about

to leave the room.

"Are you sure that you are all right going back on that Yacht?"

"Yes, sir, I'll be fine," replied Casey.

"You've been through a lot recently Casey. Don't take any unnecessary risks. Plant the surveillance devices and get off as quickly and quietly as you can," said Agent Jones as he gave him a pat on the back.

Agent Evans was waiting on Casey and Holly. She had their equipment bag complete with wetsuits and a change of clothes.

CHAPTER EIGHT

DEADLY CONSEQUENCES

Sam and Agent Jones were sitting in the Sheriff's office, working out what to say to Franco. The message would have to be put into code using Franco's cipher, and Rebecca had left to retrieve the cipher from the evidence bag over half an hour beforehand.

The door opened, and Sam had to look twice at the girl that walked through it.

"OH MY GOODNESS!" Exclaimed an astonished Sam.

"What have you done to yourself?"

"Agent Evans gave me some hair dye," replied Rebecca.

"Why would she do that?" Asked Sam.

"Because Franco has seen me and I had to change my appearance," Rebecca said calmly as she looked at her new look in a mirror on the wall.

"Mum is going to kill you," laughed Sam.

"It's not permanent and washes out, Dummy" Retorted Rebecca.

She had never had her hair dyed and quite liked how she looked with Blonde hair.

"Good thinking," said Agent Jones, without even lifting his eyes away from what he was doing on the table.

Rebecca tilted her head and gave Sam a smug smirk. Every now and then the two of them liked to revert to typical sibling bickering.

Rebecca handed Agent Jones the cipher that had been found in franco's Washington apartment.

"Sam, get ready to put this message in code," Sam nodded "I'm ready."

"Client has agreed on new terms. Send bank details."

Sam quickly began putting the text into code.

"Rebecca use Brakker's cell phone to send the message to Franco," instructed Agent Jones.

Rebecca went over to fetch the cell phone from the wall charger.

She input the numbers in the same way that they had seen the previously coded message from Franco.

"That's it sent," said Rebecca as she pressed send.

"Now we wait," said Agent Jones.

Ten minutes passed, and there had been no reply from Franco.

"When do we contact the Russians?" Enquired Sam, as he tried to break the tense silence in the room.

Agent Jones had been standing staring out of the window since the message had been sent. He thrived on the pressure of live operations and like a super-computer his mind analysed every conceivable outcome, planning their responses for each scenario. Sam's voice brought him back to them.

"We'll send Franco's bank account details when we have them, and request them to send the money immediately," replied Agent Jones.

"Rebecca, how long is that since we text him?" Asked Agent Jones, as he sat down at the table again.

He took the cipher and started using it to write down a series of numbers.

"It's just 15 minutes," replied Rebecca.

“He should have replied by now,” said a slightly worried Agent Jones.

“Rebecca, text this message to Franco.”

“OK! Go ahead,” said Rebecca, as she grabbed Brakker’s phone from the table.

Agent Jones rhymed off the sequence of numbers

“53 23 54 15 22 - 34 41 - 31 34 32 55 - 55 44 33 32 53 42 53 54 34 15.”

Sam queried the plan again with Agent Jones.

“Casey and Holly will deploy the cameras and microphones on the Yacht during the night and first thing tomorrow morning, providing Franco replies, we’ll send the Russians a message with the location for their exchange. Is that right?” Asked Sam.

“Yes, that way, we’ll hopefully know what they’re thinking and planning…” Agent Jones’s reply was interrupted by the sound of an incoming text message from Brakker’s cell phone.

The three of them stared at the sequence of numbers in the text message.

“I wish these guys would just talk normally to each other,” quipped Rebecca as she started trying to decode the message.

Sam was reading the first part of the message aloud as Rebecca wrote it down on the paper.

"Send money to my Swiss bank account."

"Brakker must know his bank details already!" Said Agent Jones.

"I wonder why he never told us?"

Rebecca finished the message. "Meet me at the Island in Boggy Creek, an hour after the money transfer."

"How are we going to know when the money has been transferred?" Asked Sam as he suddenly realised that they had no way of knowing when the Russians had paid the money.

"Don't worry about it, I'll deal with that. Time to have a word with Brakker though and find out why he's been holding out on us!" Said Agent Jones as he headed for the door.

Sam and Rebecca made their way to the Observation room and watched as Agent Jones quizzed Brakker.

"I didn't think it was relevant at the moment," said Brakker.

"In his defence, it probably wasn't," said Rebecca to Sam.

"So what are his account details?" Asked Agent Jones.

"I have them written down in my villa. But you'll need the torch from my backpack to find them," replied Brakker.

Brakker then gave Agent Jones directions to look amongst the books on a shelf in the Living room for the Washington Travel Guide.

"His bank account details are written in invisible ink on the page about the Natural History Museum," smirked Brakker.

Agent Jones was shaking his head in disbelief and remarked, "of all the places to note it!"

"I was afraid that I'd lose the details," chuckled Brakker.

Agent Jones walked to the two-way window.

"Sam, ask the Sheriff to take you."

Sam knew exactly what he meant and went to get the Sheriff.

Agent Jones returned to speak with Brakker.

"How do we communicate with the Russians?"

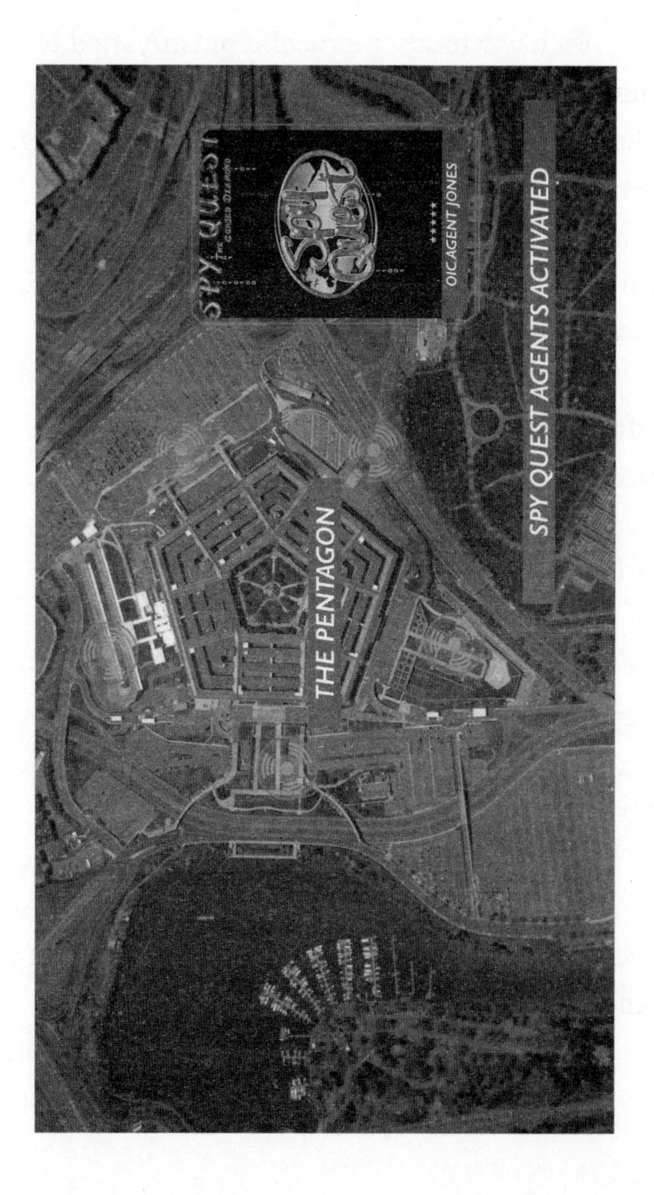
SPY QUEST!
OIC.AGENT JONES
THE PENTAGON
SPY QUEST AGENTS ACTIVATED

"They use another type of cipher. A copy of it is in my photos on my phone." Agent Jones took Brakker's phone from his pocket and asked him to find it.

"Have they sent you any money yet?" Asked Agent Jones.

Brakker hesitated.

"Whatever you're thinking, you need to be truthful with me or you're going straight to jail," warned Agent Jones.

Brakker let out a large sigh. "They've paid me the original million already."

"And, you weren't going to tell us that?" Snapped an unhappy Agent Jones.

"I need your bank account details and access to your account so that we can electronically transfer money from your account."

Brakker nodded his head in agreement and took the pen that Agent Jones handed him and wrote down his account details, as well as, his password for his online account.

Agent Jones then made his way back into the Observation room.

"Rebecca, I need you to prepare a money transfer of $1,000,000 from Brakker's account to Franco's account. Speak with Sam and get the account details from him. Don't send it just yet."

Rebecca nodded in acknowledgement and went to find a laptop from Agent Jones' car.

Sam was sitting in the front seat of the Sheriff's car. He was a bit small to be sitting in the front of such a big car and had to stretch himself up so that he could see over the huge dashboard.

The Sheriff hadn't been to the resort or villa before, and Sam was directing him.

Sam was peering over the dashboard and couldn't believe his eyes when he saw Ivan and Halina walking out of the side entrance to Brakker's villa.

"Keep driving, keep driving past." Sam shouted to the Sheriff as he ducked down in the seat.

They must have forced entry into the villa looking for Brakker and the last thing they would want was for a Sheriff's car to pass them as they came out. He thought as he looked at the Sheriff.

"Don't draw attention to us. Just act naturally

and don't look at them."

Sam reflected on that last comment. *Just act naturally!*

Possibly not the best choice of words. Surely, the natural thing for a Sheriff to do was to give chase and catch someone who had just broken into a villa.

Sam was relieved to see the Sheriff react to this and look the other way as they drove past the villa.

He peeked his head up and watched out of the rear window.

Ivan and Halina must have been thanking their lucky stars and weren't hanging about to have a conversation with the local Sheriff. Sam watched as they drove off around the corner.

"Just stop here please and I'll go back on foot," instructed Sam.

The Sheriff pulled into a line of cars and Sam hopped out.

He jogged back to the villa and found that the door hadn't been forced. *They must just have been looking for Brakker and went around the rear to see if he was inside*, he thought.

Once inside he quickly located the Washington

Travel Guide and found the page that Brakker was referring to.

"There's nothing on it," he murmured as he checked either side of the pages.

"Ah, the torch."

Sam had forgotten about the torch from Brakker's backpack.

He located it and promptly shone the Ultra Violet light of the torch at the page, where it revealed a list of coded numbers.

Not more codes, Sam thought as he called Rebecca.

Sam read over the numbers to Rebecca, and she started to decode them.

"OYAK Anker Bank. Account No 0019671506."

"Great, get yourself back here quickly. I'm just about to message the Russians and ask for the nine million to be paid into Brakker's account immediately."

"They've just left here, I saw them snooping around the villa looking for Brakker" warned Sam.

He then locked up the villa and ran back to the Sheriff's car.

Rebecca tapped the window to the interview room to get Agent Jones's attention and he then joined her in the Observation room.

"Sam got the account details, and I've prepared the wire transfer to Franco's account."

Agent Jones paused for a moment to collect his thoughts.

"Okay, send the money and message Franco to say that the remainder will be paid when Brakker sees the diamond at Boggy Creek."

"Then message the Russians with the coded message to ask for the nine million to be paid into Brakker's account within the next hour or the deal is off."

"Okay," said Rebecca as she hit the computer button to send the wire transfer.

"Once you've sent the messages I'll meet you out in the rear yard," said Agent Jones as he went to get Brakker ready.

Rebecca was busy coding the message for the Russians when she received a message on Brakker's cell phone. She could feel butterflies in her stomach as she went to read what it said.

It was from Franco. No coded messages this time, just a simple "OK."

"The clock is ticking," she said under her breath. She could feel the nervous excitement building within her and the butterflies were turning to full on stomach churning.

She finished her coded message and sent it to the Russians.

Even if they don't bite, we'll still have the diamond and Franco, she thought, as she silently congratulated herself.

Rebecca found Agent Jones seated within a large Black SUV, in the rear yard and to her surprise, Sam was already back and in the rear seat. Brakker was seated slumped and looking dejected in the front passenger's seat.

She climbed in and gave everyone the good news about Franco.

Rebecca then noticed that Agent Jones had changed his clothing and now looked a bit like a hobo. He was wearing an old, slightly torn t-shirt which he'd borrowed from the Sheriff. It had "Boggy Creek Airboats" logo on the chest. Boggy Creek was only a twenty-minute car ride from the Sheriff's Office. Sam and Rebecca both thought it was the longest twenty minutes of their lives.

The creek itself was a local tourist attraction and several vendors hired airboats by the hour so that tourists could go out into the creek and see alligators in their natural environment. It was too dangerous for anyone to enter the water or even get too close to the water's edge. Jetty's ran from the embankment out into the water to allow tourists to safely board the airboats. Nobody said anything the whole journey to the North side of the creek.

Agent Jones was going to accompany Brakker to the island in the middle of the creek. Sam and Rebecca were to hang about the main pier and watch for Franco arriving.

The FBI were on standby a little distance away from the Creek. Once Franco was seen, Agent Jones would alert them and they would swoop in to arrest him.

Sounds a simple plan, thought Sam.

Rebecca was a bit unsure. Things never seemed

to go quite the way you expect.

Agent Jones hired an airboat and they sailed off towards the island in the middle. He was acting as Brakker's Airboat driver.

"Cool disguise," said Sam as he put his sunglasses on.

"Let's look for Franco," he added as he surveyed the nearby cafe and boat hire stalls.

Rebecca had grabbed a pair of binoculars from the kit bag and was still watching Agent Jones as they landed on the island. A long wooden Jetty stretched from the creek over a small beach and onto the grassy island where it met a gravel path which, split right and left circling the island.

"I can watch them from here; do you want to have a look around?" She asked Sam.

"OMG, I can see the alligators, the creek is full of them," she exclaimed as she watched Agent Jones tie the airboat to the end of the Jetty.

"Let me see," said Sam as he grabbed the binoculars from Rebecca.

Rebecca gave Sam a hard push.

"They're still attached, you know," she said as

she removed the strap from over her head.

"Sorry. I didn't realise," said Sam with a slight smile.

Sam could see the alligators crawling up the sandy beach towards the grass at the side of the Jetty.

"They're huge," he said in amazement.

"Luckily, they don't seem too bothered about humans. They just want to lie in the sunshine," added Rebecca as she took the binoculars back.

"Right I'm off," said Sam as he went to look around and see if he could find Franco.

Rebecca stood watching Agent Jones and Brakker standing on the jetty.

To her astonishment, she watched as Brakker turned and suddenly punched Agent Jones in the face. The force caught Agent Jones by surprise which gave Brakker time to grab him and throw him off the side of the Jetty towards the alligators.

"SAM!" Screamed Rebecca.

Sam turned around and came running back toward Rebecca.

"What is it?" He shouted as he approached her.

"Brakker is trying to Kill Agent Jones!"

Screamed Rebecca.

"The alligators are trying to bite him," said Rebecca with tears in her eyes.

"Sam, I can't watch."

She handed the binoculars to Sam and put her head in her hands.

Sam quickly looked through the binoculars.

There was no sign of Brakker and Agent Jones was on the ground scrambling to get to his feet as about eight alligators were closing in on him. The only trouble was, Agent Jones had nowhere to go. He was at the water's edge and the alligators were in between him, the island and the Jetty.

"He's a sitting Duck," said Sam to Rebecca. "Is he dead?" Asked Rebecca.

Sam looked around for inspiration. He then shoved the binoculars back in Rebecca's hands and began to run off towards an Airboat that was just coming into the Pier.

"Cancel Franco," Sam shouted to Rebecca.

Rebecca knew what Sam meant and quickly started texting Franco. She didn't use code. There was no time.

Her message had to help stop Franco in his tracks and put him off coming to the Creek but at the same time not cause him to think something was up.

"Cancel meeting. Police everywhere as someone bitten by Gator."

Perfect, she thought.

"Let's hope he's not here yet," she said under her breath.

Sam went sprinting across to an airboat that was docked and ready to go out on its next excursion. He darted past the queue of people that were waiting to board.

"My Dad's in trouble," he shouted as he jumped into the drivers seat.

"Take this," said an elderly man, as he threw his walking stick into the boat.

Everyone realised the dangers in the Creek and the man had been quick to realise that Sam was going to rescue someone and not just stealing the boat.

"How hard can this be?" Said Sam to himself as he grabbed the lever on his left. Since they'd arrived he'd been watching some of the other drivers; one stick, forward for right, back for left. "Easy!" He said.

He turned the ignition on and swept the boat round to face the island.

The confidence that he'd gained from his training was immense. He wasn't afraid to do anything and embraced every challenge with vigour.

He could see the alligators snapping at Agent Jones as they got closer to him. There was no way around them and he was a dead man if he tried to swim away from them too.

"Kevin! Kevin! Kevin!" Sam shouted repeatedly, at the top of his voice.

Agent Jones turned to see Sam approaching on the Airboat.

Sam still didn't actually have a plan. He was headed straight for Agent Jones at high speed but wasn't sure what he was actually going to do or how he was going to rescue him. He gazed at the walking stick that the man had thrown into the boat.

Pfft! That would be like a toothpick to an alligator, he thought as he desperately tried to come up with something. Anything!

Sam was now sixty yards from the island and travelling at full ramming speed towards the beach.

Perhaps, I could take them out like a bowling ball hitting the pins and jump out in time to escape, he contemplated.

"Oh NO! What are you doing?" He shouted, as he watched Agent Jones suddenly dive into the water.

Rebecca was watching again on the shore and she nearly fainted when she saw Agent Jones dive into the water. The alligators must have thought it was their lucky day.

Immediately, every gator that was lying on the banking, started waddling towards the water.

Sam suddenly realised that there was no brake; he remembered 'Newton's Laws of Motion' and pulled the lever backwards sharply, in an attempt to slow it down in case he went right over the top of Agent Jones.

He watched intently for any sign of him in the water. Was it too late? Had the Gators already in the water caught him and pulled him to the bottom of the dark water.

Just then, Agent Jones surfaced. He had travelled quite a bit underwater and was now swimming like a man possessed towards Sam.

The alligators from the beach were in the water

now and covering ground fast. Sam could see the eyes of at least five alligators who were close behind him. Their long tails frantically propelled them forward at great speed and for a moment they reminded him of an excited dog wagging its tail ready for its dinner.

The boat began to slow and Sam leapt out of the chair and went to help Agent Jones aboard. Sam grabbed the walking stick and reached out to him as he neared the boat.

Agent Jones grabbed the stick and pulled himself up to the side of the boat.

Sam was frantically grabbing his clothes and trying to get him inside when the first gator came swimming rapidly towards them. Agent Jones left leg was still submerged in the water.

There was no time for thinking. Instinctively, Sam grabbed the stick and swung it right at the eyes of the Gator. With all his strength, he smacked it right on the head. The ferocity of the strike broke the walking stick in two.

The force of the strike deterred the alligator and to Sam's relief it disappeared underneath the boat.

With Agent Jones now safely onboard, Sam

asked "Are you all right?" As he looked over his body for any blood.

"I'm fine, I'm fine. Thank you Sam," said a very relieved and out of breath Agent Jones.

Sam jumped back in the driver's seat and headed for the island Jetty. He now had time to communicate with Rebecca on the radio and asked if she had been watching. She said that she had seen the whole thing and was still shaking.

"Have you seen Brakker?" Questioned Sam.

"He disappeared out of sight on the path to the left of the island and hasn't come back," replied Rebecca.

"There's only one way on and one way off the island," said Agent Jones as he pulled himself up to his feet.

"Now let's go get him."

Sam tied the boat up at the end of the Jetty and they both climbed up onto the wooden planks above. Agent Jones took a moment to wring out his wet t-shirt, before they walked past the now deserted beach.

"I think the Gators were expecting a feast" quipped Sam as saw Agent Jones survey the beach and look out to the Creek.

"They'd probably have spat me back out," replied Agent Jones with a wry smile.

"Right, he's probably thought he could get off the island and will be making his way around it," said Agent Jones with a look of revenge in his eyes.

"Should we call in the FBI now?" Asked Sam.

"No, let's try to find him first. He won't be so lucky this time..,"

Rebecca interrupted them. "Agent Jones, I cancelled Franco and he's just text back to ask for a rescheduled meeting time."

"Well done, Rebecca. Keep your eyes on the island and warn us if you see Brakker," he instructed, as he motioned for Sam to follow him.

"We'll go to the right and hopefully, he'll walk straight into us," said Agent Jones as he strode off with determination.

Sam was amazed at how quickly Agent Jones regained his composure. Moments ago he'd nearly died and now he was like Captain America and off in hunt of his target.

They hadn't gotten far when Rebecca shouted

over the radio,

"I see him, I see him," she screamed a bit too loudly.

"Quick he must have been watching you heading in the opposite direction and he's now running towards the airboats."

Agent Jones and Sam sprinted back towards the jetty and could see Brakker running towards it too. He was much closer and was going to reach the boat before them.

Brakker ran full speed onto the jetty, making his way to Sam's airboat.

"Oh No!" Cried Sam, as he searched his pocket for the keys to the boat.

"I've left the keys in the ignition," he shouted at Agent Jones who was now ten yards ahead of him.

They watched helplessly as he neared the boat. He was going to be too far ahead of them to catch him.

As Brakker approached the airboat he tried to stop running and lost his footing on the slippy wet boards.

"He's not going to make it," shouted Sam.

The three Agents watched in horror as Brakker slid straight off the end of the Jetty and into the water.

Sam and Agent Jones couldn't see him in the water from their position. He had just disappeared over the edge.

Rebecca watched in disbelief as she saw him hit the water. She saw him surface once, before he disappeared back underneath for the final time.

Every Gator in the Creek had been near to the Island from the recent events and finally their wishes had been granted. They weren't about to let another dinner get away so easily.

AGENT

CHAPTER NINE

NIGHT OPS

Agent Evans drove Casey and Holly down to Tampa. On the way Casey filled Holly in on the layout of the Yacht and possible positions for them to plant their devices.

They decided that they would wait until the middle of the night before swimming over to the Yacht. An hour or so later and they were back at the Marina. Casey looked around with a feeling of Déjà vu.

"No sign of their SUV," said Casey as he looked for their vehicle. "And, their Yacht is further out to sea."

"I wonder why that is?" Remarked Holly.

"Maybe they think it would be harder for someone to swim out to it," replied Casey as he peered through the binoculars.

They gazed around for the best advantage point to watch the movements of the people on the Yacht.

"Let's try there," said Agent Evans pointing to a large, elegant looking hotel building which was located on the far side of the Marina.

They drove over, and Agent Evans went in to make enquiries.

A short time later and they were all within a penthouse room at the top of the hotel.

"What a view!" Remarked Holly as she looked out at the beautiful aqua blue water, which stretched as far as the eye could see into the horizon.

Agent Evans began setting up a large camera lens in the living room.

"You two go get some rest and I'll finish setting up here," she instructed.

The penthouse had two bedrooms.

"The master suite is the size of my parents house," said Casey as he walked through the bedroom and into the massive en-suite bathroom.

"That's why I'm sleeping here," laughed Holly as she jumped on the King size bed.

"No! No! You know the drill. Go…Rock… Paper…Scissors…"

Casey left Holly starfished on the massive bed and went to explore his room.

"Have you seen the size of the walk-in wardrobes? We could throw a party in them alone!" Shouted Holly after him.

The second room was obviously meant for the children and was almost as big as the master, with a large 60-inch flat-screen TV on the wall and a state of the art surround sound.

Casey found a wireless games controller and a control pad the size of a tablet but there was no sign of a games console.

He started pressing random buttons on the control pad to see what happened. He smiled to himself as the curtains began closing, lights flicked on and off and the Air-con burred, as a cold air shot through the vents. A loud blast of music briefly, interrupted his exploration.

"Casey, turn that down," shouted Agent Evans.

"Sorry! Didn't mean that," he shouted back.

"That'll be the Music system," he murmured

under his breath.

"Now what does this do," he said as he pressed the last button.

He looked around to see if anything had happened.

Nothing! He thought, surprised that he still hadn't found the games machine.

He decided to give up and walked over to the bed. To his surprise, he noticed that the side of the cabinet beside the bed had opened. He peered in and was pleased to see the familiar sight of his favourite games machine.

Cool! He thought, as he jumped down and opened the door of the cabinet. Inside was a vast collection of games.

"What to play, what to play?" He said as he pondered over which game to play.

NHL NFL, COD, Minecraft. Some classics here. Meant to be chilling, he thought as he decided on a game of FIFA.

Agent Evans was busy setting up the technical equipment in the living room; The huge tele-photo lens on the camera was directed at the Yacht and the camera had a direct link of live footage to be relayed back to Head Quarters. Sat beside the camera was a laser designator, which marked the GPS position of the Yacht. The designator provided an invisible laser beam that fired a series of coded pulses which bounce off the target and into the sky. This enabled the Agency to direct one of their Spy Satellites to watch it from Space.

Spy satellites circle the earth in the Low Earth Orbit (LEO). This means that they have an altitude of between 100 - 1,240 miles above the Earth. The satellites are that powerful that they can be used to read the newspaper of anyone down below.

Despite her comfy bed, Holly couldn't sleep and went to see if anything was happening on the Yacht.

As she opened the door, Agent Evans was looking through the viewfinder on the camera, but to Holly's surprise, she was pointing it down below and not out at the Yacht.

"Standby, Standby, Standby," barked Agent Evans.

Holly grabbed a pair of binoculars and rushed over to the window.

Agent Evans was watching an SUV that had just

entered the Marina car park. The occupants were still inside the vehicle.

She was hoping to get good images of them so that face recognition could identify them.

"Holly, quickly turn the TV on," said Agent Evans.

Holly put the TV on, and it lit up with the live action from the camera feed. Agent Evans had connected a cable from it to the TV, so that they could watch it on the big screen.

They watched as Ivan and Halina got out of the vehicle and headed along the jetty towards the small boat that they kept docked there.

"Gotcha!" Whispered Agent Evans as she pressed the shutter button of the camera to capture still images of them.

"Brilliant, you managed to get them face on!" Exclaimed Holly as the images appeared on the big screen.

"Yes, they're nice clear images, we should be able to identify them easily if they are on file. HQ are receiving the live stream and we will see what they come back with," said Agent Evans.

Both of them watched Ivan and Halina approach the yacht, this time there were four armed guards walking up and down the decks.

As they climbed aboard, they were warmly greeted by an older man, who approved from within the cabin. The three of them chatted for a few moments before they settled themselves down on the seated area of the lower deck. A short time later a maid brought them all drinks and food.

"Doesn't look like they're going anywhere soon, you need to get some sleep before tonight."

"I know, I'm a bit tired now," said Holly as she headed back to her room.

Casey and Holly managed to get some sleep and as darkness fell, Agent Evans woke them up and asked them to join her in the living room, where she broke the news about what had happened to Brakker at the Creek. Both of them were shocked that Brakker had attempted to flee and relieved that Agent Jones and Sam were safe.

Agent Evans settled herself on the sofa and placed the laptop on the coffee table in front of her. She used her access code to login to the Spy Quest

Agencies secure web site and immediately, the picture of Ivan appeared on the TV. This time however, he was in military uniform.

"That's Ivan," exclaimed Casey.

"Ivan Semak, aged 35, born in Omsk, which is a city in South Western Siberia. Former Russian special forces, now retired and a soldier of fortune," said Agent Evans.

"A what?" Asked Holly.

'Soldiers of Fortune' are usually ex-military personnel, who sell their unique professional services to the highest bidders."

Agent Evans then hit the enter button on the laptop and the picture of Halina appeared on the big screen.

"That's Halina," confirmed Casey.

"Halina Kirichenko, aged 33, also born in Omsk. She retired from the military in the same year as Ivan and is also a mercenary," said Agent Evans.

"Do we know who they are working for now?" Asked Casey.

"Yes! This man," replied Agent Evans as she brought up the next picture.

"This is General Nikolai Belenov, he's actually a retired Russian General but still uses his old title. Former head of the old KGB and now a retired Billionaire who spends all his time aboard his luxury Yacht," said Agent Evans, as she pointed out towards the Yacht.

"Belenov, has some extreme views and has his own private army made up of soldiers who used to serve under him. He is highly dangerous!"

"Is he an art or jewel collector?" Asked Holly.

"Not to our knowledge," replied Agent Evans.

"Why would he want the Hope Diamond?" Said Casey thoughtfully, as he walked over to look out of the window.

"Doesn't make sense!" Added Holly.

"Well, hopefully we're about to find out. Time to get ready," said Agent Evans, as she brought everyone's attention back to the current mission.

"Oxygen tanks are in the boot of the car. Take these. New bits of kit that will help you hear me better," said Agent Evans as she handed them both a small earpiece.

"Waterproof earpieces! Excellent, could have

done with these the last time I was at the Yacht," said Casey as he put on his earpiece.

Casey and Holly used the rear stairwell and had a blanket wrapped around them in case they bumped into anyone. They made their way over to the SUV and got ready to go.

Both of them had a small waterproof bag; Holly's contained four listening devices which were to be put in and around the seated area on the deck and inside the main living room area of the Yacht. Casey's bag contained a small camera; this was to be positioned at the rear of the Yacht and would allow them to see the people onboard and help identify who was talking.

In his bag, he also had a GPS tracker with a special mount that could be attached to the fibreglass hull of the Yacht. The tracker would emit a signal at regular intervals to provide the whereabouts of the Yacht anywhere in the world, at any given time.

Casey and Holly walked down to the end of the jetty. A half-moon was hidden by thick clouds, leaving the Marina in complete darkness.

"A storm is brewing," remarked Casey to Holly,

as he looked up at the clouds.

"Let's get this done before it breaks," replied Holly as she winced after looking at the dark skies.

They sat down at the edge of the jetty, their legs dangling over. One last check.

"Come in Casey, can you hear me?" Asked Agent Evans.

"Loud and clear," replied Casey.

"Come in Holly, can you hear me" asked Agent Evans.

"Loud and clear too," replied Holly.

"Receiving you both well. Good luck," said Agent Evans signing off.

Casey and Holly slipped silently into the water.

They swam side by side using the Dive Scooters. Holly loved using the Dive Scooters, she broke off from Casey and began mimicking how Dolphins swim, by pointing the Dive Scooter deeper into the water and then quickly pulling it upwards repeatedly.

Casey smiled to himself, he knew what Holly was doing. *That girl wished she was a dolphin*, he thought as he followed her towards the Yacht.

They both slowed up and drifted towards the

rear of the Yacht, careful not to cause too much of a ripple in the water. Claps of thunder could be heard in the distance and the moon provided occasional chinks of light on the decking.

Casey remained in the water and began trying to find somewhere to place his GPS Tracker.

Holly could feel her heart pounding and was sure it was about to burst through her chest as she emerged silently from the water and slid down to lie on the deck next to the seated area at the rear.

She waited a few moments before crawling around to find the best place to hide the microphones. The single seats looked like a good place and she tilted one over to look at the fabric underneath.

Perfect, she thought as she examined the stitching at the sides closely. She took a small sharp knife from her utility belt and cut a small slit in the stitching. It was enough for her to put her small hand in. She took a microphone from the bag and placed it within the interior of the seat. The microphones had a sticky backing, which allowed them to be stuck onto wood.

"Simply remove the backing and hold tight

on the surface for ten seconds," repeated Holly as she remembered her instructions from training.

She let go and gave the device a tug.

Solid!

She then repeated the same thing on the other single seat.

"Boo," said Casey as he crept up on Holly.

"Huh, Huh!" Gasped Holly as she tried to stop herself from screaming.

Holly hadn't heard Casey coming and wasn't too pleased at him giving her a fright.

She gave Casey a death stare and was wishing that she could also punch him.

Casey knew exactly what was going through Holly's mind and gave her a cheeky smirk and wink, before heading back to the rear of the Yacht to look for a good spot for the Camera.

Holly finished up on the deck and then went to the doors to the living room area. She wasn't looking forward to this, as it was the most dangerous part of the mission. The curtains were pulled and she couldn't see within.

She had to wait till Casey finished, so that both

of them could make a quick getaway if they needed to.

Holly heard a "Beep, Beep, Beep." through her earpiece and knew that it was the signal from Casey's communication device to say that he was ready.

Gently she pulled on the sliding door and was pleased that it wasn't locked. It slid effortlessly open, just enough for her to slip inside. The room was in darkness and it was hard to see anything. Holly didn't have infrared glasses with her and had to wait till her eyes adjusted.

I could do with the moonlight now, she thought just as a streak of lightning lit the room up. She waited on her eyes to readjust to the darkness. It was a large open plan room with kitchen, dining and seating areas. She quickly scanned the kitchen area but couldn't find anywhere suitable to hide the device.

Holly moved over behind the large sofa and was reaching under it when the radio suddenly crackled into life.

"Standby, Standby, Standby," said Agent Evans, in a whispered voice.

Holly froze and waited for the next update. She couldn't hear anything, but then again she hadn't heard

Casey creeping up behind her earlier.

Agent Evans voice came over the radio again.

"A light has come on in the lower.....

The storm outside was right above them now and the sound of the thunder drowned out Agent Evans last words. Holly suddenly realised what Agent Evans was trying to communicate to them. To her horror, she now heard footsteps coming towards her.

The thunder had drowned out their approach and now someone was almost upon her position...

She looked over at the sliding door through which she had entered considering her escape.

Oh, No! She thought.

She had left the door open, not much, but enough for the wind to blow the curtain ever so slightly.

It was too late now, there was nothing that could be done about it; if she moved, she would certainly be discovered and possibly captured.

Now lying down behind the sofa she quickly edged herself closer to the back of it, holding her breath as a dark figure passed right by where she lay.

She could not see who it was that had entered the living area but for now was more concerned with not being discovered herself. The fridge door opened, lighting the room a little, and she could hear someone rummaging through the refrigerator.

She glanced over at the open door again and saw it start to close very slowly.

Casey! She thought as she lay there hoping that the figure would not glance round while the refrigerator door was still open.

Casey had heard the warning from Agent Evans, he wasn't about to leave his friend behind and was now standing just outside the door in case Holly needed him. And she did.

The rain and the wind were getting heavier as the storm progressed and he knew there was every chance that whoever it was in the room with Holly, could discover the open door and alert the sleeping guards. So he waited until he was sure that the figure was busy in the refrigerator and using the sound of the storm to mask any sound he made, before he closed the sliding door.

Holly heard the fridge door close and let out her

breath in a slight sigh of relief as she heard the footsteps get further away. This time, she heard the room door close.

"The light below deck has now been extinguished," came Agent Evans' voice over the radio.

She was none the wiser as to what had just happened.

Holly finished up and joined Casey outside.

"You OK?" Whispered Casey.

"Yes, thanks," smiled Holly.

"Fab, let's get out of here," said Casey as they crouched down and crept to the back of the Yacht.

CHAPTER TEN
THE EXCHANGE

After their unsuccessful search for Brakker, Sam and Agent Jones returned to the shore. The Police had arrived and whilst Agent Jones briefed them on what had happened, Sam, and Rebecca returned to the SUV; it was getting late and it had been an eventful day.

"I think we'll call it a day and head back to the training base. It's getting late," said Agent Jones as he joined the pair in the car.

"It's been an eventful day."

"Sure has!" Said Sam.

"It's not over yet!" Announced Rebecca as she checked Brakker's messages. "The Russians have paid the money!"

"Great, we'll arrange the exchanges for

tomorrow and give everyone time to get some rest tonight," said Agent Jones as he drove them back to the Orlando training camp.

Just as they arrived back, Rebecca received another coded message from Franco.

"We'll head to the operations room and decode it there," said Agent Jones.

Once inside the building, they all gathered around and Rebecca started to decode the message.

"Sam, read it back to me," said Rebecca.

"No need, watch this!" Said Sam, as he launched Holly's Spy Cam App and then held his cell phone over the message.

Right away, the Spy Cam started to decode the message.

The numbers "25 44 44 53 - 54 15 - 32 52 54 34 42 - 15 34 34 15." changed to reveal the secret message.

"Awesome!" Exclaimed Rebecca.

"No! Not awesome! Declared Agent Jones.

"That is NOT a good place for an exchange."

"Surely, it means that he can't get in carrying a firearm," said Sam.

"And there is only one way in and one way out," added Rebecca.

"There is too many people; it will be a logistical nightmare trying to track him. Although, I suppose it is fully covered with CCTV, and we can use that to our advantage," replied Agent Jones as he grimaced at the tough decision he had to make.

"Okay, text him back to agree with the location and time,"

Rebecca nodded in agreement.

"Then tell the Russians that their exchange will be at 4 pm tomorrow and location to follow."

"Will do."

"Now, you two get some sleep and we'll meet back here at 9 am," said Agent Jones before he went off to make the arrangements for the exchanges.

Next morning, Sam and Rebecca heard a knock on their door. Sam opened the door and in burst Casey with Holly following behind. He grabbed Sam in a headlock.

"Well done, my little Padawan. I heard how

well you did yesterday." he said as he rapidly rubbed his hair.

He looked up to see the look he was getting from Rebecca. Letting go of Sam, he reached out to Rebeca to repeat the action on her.

"Eh, no!" Rebecca said. "A simple well done will do!"

"Sorry, how well you both did," he corrected his statement.

"Better," said Rebecca as she started to smile.

"How did you both get on?" Rebecca asked Holly.

Holly told them about nearly being discovered and how dangerous it was swimming back to shore in the storm.

"OMG! I would have needed to go to the toilet after that," said Rebecca.

Casey was buzzing.

"I can't believe we're going to get Franco and the Russian's in one day," said Casey.

"8 am, we better get some breakfast first," said Holly as she looked at her watch.

An hour later and they were all sat in the Operational Briefing room waiting for Agent Jones.
The room started to fill with FBI Agents.

"I didn't expect us to need so many people," said Casey with surprise in his voice. He gazed around and gave a wave to a few people that he knew.

"Who are they?" Asked Sam.

"FBI," replied Casey.

"Why are they wearing refuse collectors and car park attendant uniforms?"

"Agent Jones must have asked for their help in backing us up. Probably not taking any chances after yesterday," Casey added.

Agent Jones entered the room and took up a position at the lectern in the middle of the stage. The big screen behind him sprung to life and the picture of Franco appeared.

"Ladies and Gentlemen," barked Agent Jones, to get silence in the room.

Agent Jones went on to brief everyone on the background of the case and what their responsibilities were during the mission; they were to catch Franco at the first exchange and once they had him and the diamond, they would intercept the Russian's at the second rendevous.

Agent Jones informed everyone that the exchange with the Russians was to take place in the car park of a disused retail outlet at 4 pm. A satellite image of the car park appeared on the screen and he then pointed out the positions for the strike teams to take.

At the end of the briefing, everyone started to file out of the building and into the waiting unmarked transport vans.

Agent Jones beckoned for the four young agents to join him on the stage.

"You'll all come with me. Rebecca, you are still in charge of Brakker's cell phone and the ciphers."

"Okay," replied Rebecca.

"When we go into the theme park, you'll all act as tourists enjoying your vacation but keep each other in view."

"Clear?"

"Yes Sir," they all replied, before heading off to the theme park.

Sam and Rebecca were really excited to go inside

the park. They had hoped to make time to visit at least one theme park while they were in Orlando training but hadn't expected to be working on a live operation at the time.

Driving up the I4 Freeway, Casey was pointing out his favourite rides from all the 3D billboards at the side of the roadway.

"My favourite is the Super Heroes land. They have one of the best roller coasters there," said Casey as they passed a billboard for the latest Super Heroes roller coaster.

"Although, I haven't been on that one yet," he added.

"If it all goes to plan, I might let you all stay on tonight," said Agent Jones.

They all gave each other an excited glance.

Sam could see the tall structures of the roller coasters getting closer and closer. He could feel the excitement building within him.

I hope this goes well and we're finished quickly, he thought.

Agent Jones pulled off the Freeway at junction 75A and was following the signs for the theme park, car park.

Rebecca was enjoying the scenery just as much as Sam. She was surprised at the long line of cars waiting in line at the ticket booths and expected it to take a long time to get through the gates. The efficiency of the attendants in getting cars through the gates surprised her. All the other park visitors cars headed left and Agent Jones turned right towards the security and staff area. The three unmarked FBI transit vans followed closely behind.

They all parked their vehicles in a line and the FBI Agents made their way immediately from their vans and into the park, to take up their positions.

They were all dressed in the staff uniforms for the theme park. Once through the gates Sam and Rebecca watched them scatter in different directions; some were litter pickers, others were to be balloon sellers, and there were even some that dressed as photographers.

Agent Jones spoke to one of the park's security team and then came back over to talk to them.

"I'll be in the control room to monitor all the surveillance cameras. Put your earpieces in and always wear you sunglasses. That way, I can see what you see too."

They all acknowledged Agent Jones and gave each other a hug.

"Right lets go," said Casey as he assumed control.

They walked over to a large gate and the security guard opened it to let them slip through.

"Argh!" Squeaked Rebecca as she found herself face to face with a life-size dinosaur head.

"WOW! It's as though we've been transported back in time to the land of the Dinosaurs," said Sam as he stood staring in amazement at the huge Dinosaurs towering above them.

"Wait till you see the land of the Wizards," said Casey with a glint in his eye.

"We'll head over towards the entrance and try to get a position, so that the Face Recon can pick up Franco as he makes his way into the park," said Casey.

"I've never seen so many people in the one place," said Rebecca as they pushed their way through the crowds.

"There are too many," moaned Holly as she tried to focus on the faces of individuals funnelling through the gates and into the park.

Casey was busy looking about for a good position to get a clear look at peoples faces.

"Let's head for the bridge underneath the roller coaster," he said.

As they arrived at the wooden bridge the coaster had just taken off and the noise of it as it made its twists and turns was deafening. Sam could hardly hear anyone talking on the radio and tried to indicate this to Casey by pointing to his ear and the coaster above.

Casey knew what Sam meant and beckoned for everyone to gather around him. He knew that it was going to be difficult with the noise in the park and the sheer volume of people however, it was the best position for the Face Recon to work and he wanted to explain why he had chosen the bridge, despite the noise.

"The bridge funnels everyone through and is the only location that we can cover this amount of people all at once."

"Holly, you take the right-hand side of the

bridge, Sam you take the left-hand side, and I'll take the middle. Face towards the gates and hopefully one of us should be able to pick him up," instructed Casey.

Sam and Holly nodded in agreement.

"What about me?" Asked Rebecca.

"You will need to monitor Brakker's phone.

Grab a seat over there beside the restrooms and make sure that you can get a view of us," said Casey nodding over in the direction of the benches.

Rebecca had no problem finding a seat, as most of them were now empty. Many of the families seemed to be leaving the area all at once and heading in the same direction further in to the Super Hero attractions area. She found a table next to the restrooms and made sure that she could see them all from her position.

"Rebecca, can you hear me?" Asked Agent Jones.

"Go ahead Agent Jones," she replied.

"I can't reach Casey, Holly or Sam. Are they having any radio problems?" Quizzed Agent Jones.

"Not really! It's just that they are underneath the roller coaster and can't hear very well," replied Rebecca.

"It's the only position that they can get to use

the Face Recon," she added.

"Roger," said Agent Jones.

Rebecca took Brakker's cell phone out and placed it on the table. She looked at her watch, 11.40 am. Twenty minutes to go.

Her radio crackled again. It was Agent Jones but this time, she couldn't hear him either as the roller coaster was twisting and turning again.

She got up and started to walk away from the bench so that she could listen to what he was saying.

"Rebecca, Rebecca, can you hear me?"

"Yes, go ahead," she replied.

"We have a situation. Intelligence from the Yacht indicates that the Russians have been searching for Franco!"

"Do you understand?"

"Do you hear me?" Said Agent Jones.

"Russians are searching for Franco?" Asked Rebecca, wanting to make sure that she had heard right.

Rebecca was continuing to walk away from the bridge but found it hard to hear anything, she had walked straight into the middle of a character meet and greet in Super Hero Land and the noise of the roller coaster was now replaced with the noise of sirens and loud music coming from the large speakers that are positioned around the streets.

So this is where everyone was heading to, she thought to herself, as she tried to find a quieter spot to hear the radio. She was forced to keep to the sidewalk as the road was closed off to the public, to allow the characters to arrive on quad bikes.

"Rebecca, warn the others," shouted Agent Jones.

"Rebecca! Rebecca! Can you hear me! They intend on killing Franco and taking the diamond. Do you hear me?"

Rebecca thought that her earpiece was faulty and had taken it out to examine it.

She looked up at a security camera overhead and gave a shrug, hoping that Agent Jones would see her and send someone with a replacement. There was nothing more she could do, so turned to walk back to her seat, when an alert flashed up on her sunglasses screen.

"IDENTITY CONFIRMED, FRANCO RODRIGUEZ."

"What?" She murmured as she turned around to see where he was.

It can't be. I never saw him! She thought.

A picture of Franco then popped up on her screen.

"OMG!" Said Rebecca in total shock. Franco was dressed as a Security Guard, and had a gun. She pulled herself up onto the side of a lamppost and scanned the area for him.

There he is. She caught site of him walking away from her and further into the park.

Rebecca's Face Recon alert activated on everyone's system. Casey turned to scan the seated area for Franco and for the first time realised that Rebecca had gone.

"Rebecca where are you? What's your position?" Quizzed Casey.

Sam was beginning to panic. He tried to reach her on the radio.

"Rebecca can you hear me? Where are you?"

Casey grabbed Sam's arm and reassured him.

"Don't worry, she'll be fine. You need to let Agent Jones control the radio."

"Okay," said a slightly shaken Sam, as he felt a knot start to form in the pit of his stomach. Suddenly he had a flashback to the time when Gail Torrez and Boris had kidnapped her. He hadn't thought about how he would feel if Rebecca had got into danger again and for a moment he thought he was going to be sick.

"She's a good Agent," said Holly as she came over to reassure him too.

"Franco has a gun," was all he could say to her.

The three of them began to walk fast further into the park. Casey was just ahead of them and able to hear Agent Jones on the radio.

"Come on, she is just ahead of us," shouted Casey to the others as he began to jog.

They had to be careful, as they didn't want to draw attention to themselves by running in the park when everyone else was taking it easy in the searing heat. Sam and Holly could now hear Agent Jones. He was giving Casey directions on Rebecca's location.

Agent Jones couldn't see Franco. The camera operatives were trying desperately to find him.

"Casey. Come in Casey," said Agent Jones.

"Go ahead," replied Casey as they continued to jog and look for her.

"Rebecca is entering an underground attraction, she must have eyes on the target, although we haven't located him yet on our cameras. We're about to lose her," said Agent Jones.

Sam and Holly caught up with Casey.

"Quick, she is just ahead and is going into the underground water attraction."

Just as they were heading into the entrance, Agent Jones radioed Casey again.

"Casey. Come in Casey."

"I hear you, go ahead," he replied.

"Intelligence update from the Comms on the Yacht. The Russians are following Franco and they know that he is in the theme park. They think he works here."

Casey stopped running. He was taking a minute for that intel update to sink in.

"Does that means that the Russians are here, in the park?" He asked Agent Jones.

"Yes, but it's not Ivan and Halina. The two of

them have just left the Yacht on a helicopter and are heading here too,"

"They plan on kidnapping Franco!" added a very worried Agent Jones.

"Roger," said Casey as he sprinted after Sam and Holly.

Casey's mind was racing as he thought about Rebecca. T*hat means that she's in danger! She could walk right into the Russians and be taken with Franco!*
Or worse!

Sam and Holly reached the entrance to the ride and couldn't see Rebecca amongst the sea of people waiting in line.

Meanwhile, Rebecca had caught up on Franco and had followed him deep into the underground attraction. Rather than waiting in the queue, Franco had taken the quick pass lane which was empty and led straight to the start of the ride. She realised that she might be alone with Franco and despite her training, didn't fancy her chances in a fight and kept looking behind hoping to see Sam and the others.

A park attendant was checking everyone's pass as they approached.

Rebecca realised that she didn't have a quick pass and had to think quickly.

"I'm just going to catch up with my family." she told the attendant, as she pointed at a family group just ahead. The attendant stood aside and allowed her through without question.

The area she was in now was dark and the stone floor was uneven and bumpy. In her haste, Rebecca tripped and stumbled into the line of people who were standing in the queue. Luckily, the rope barrier, which separated the lines saved her from falling completely.

The people in the line let out a gasp and tried to break her fall.

"Oh, NO!" she mumbled.

Franco had heard the commotion and was now walking back towards Rebecca. She put her head down so that he couldn't see her face.

Come on, Think Fast, she said to herself as she saw his feet right in front of her.

"Are you alright?" He asked.

Rebecca decided that she would pretend to be French and hoped that her accent together with her blonde hair would be enough for Franco not to recognise her. She lifted her head slowly and could feel the sweat pouring down her back. As she looked at him, her face filled with horror.

OH, NO! It wasn't Franco. She had followed the wrong Security Guard!

"No time to explain," she shouted to the Guard and began to sprint back up the entrance path.

She turned a corner and ran straight into Casey, Holly, and Sam who were racing down the same quick pass line.

"It wasn't him! It wasn't him!" Screamed Rebecca.

"Quick, we can't get a signal down here, we've got to alert Agent Jones," shouted Casey, as he grabbed Sam's arm and began hauling him back the way they came.

"We still haven't seen him on camera," said Agent Jones on hearing the news.

"Go back to where Rebecca saw him, he can't be far from there," he instructed.

They began to jog back, looking in every shop along the way.

"Casey, Come in Casey," said Agent Jones.

"Go ahead," replied Casey.

"Security received a call from a tourist, who reported a disruption at the rear of the 3D ride in Super Hero Land. They don't have cameras covering that area, and it's near to where Franco was last spotted."

"We'll check it out and call in the FBI if it's him," replied Casey.

"We're not splitting up this time. Let's catch him together," said Casey to the other three, as they made their way to the rear of the 3D attraction.

Agent Jones guided them to a pathway that led to the rear of the shops and the 3D attraction.

"Listen," said Sam as he stopped next to a doorway.

"I don't hear anything," said Holly.

"Exactly!" Replied Sam. "It's so quiet back here."

"There are no speakers back here, it's almost like a different world," Rebecca chipped in.

Sam nodded in agreement.

"Shhh… I heard someone shouting," warned Casey as he gestured for them to join him.

They were all standing in front of a large grey

fire door and could definitely hear raised voices from within the building. Casey gently pushed the handle down to open the door but found it being pulled back up from the other side.

Suddenly, the door flew open towards them and a Burly man filled the frame of the doorway.

"What do you kids want?" Grumbled the man in broken English.

Casey recognised him straight away… It was the Guard from the Yacht. The one that had repeatedly kicked him in the ribs. He only had a split second to decide whether to walk away and hope that he wasn't recognised or try to take the Russian by surprise.

Holly knew what was coming next and took off her sunglasses just as Casey landed a sweet Palm strike to the Russian's nose.

He had caught the giant Russian by surprise and to his amazement had knocked him clean out. The Russian came crashing through the door and landed in a heap at Casey's feet

"OMG," cried Rebecca, who wasn't expecting it at all.

Casey clambered over the fallen Russian and

into the building. He found himself in a boiler room and immediately spotted Franco lying on the floor with a large man looming over him. It was the guard from the yacht, who had shot him. He wasted no time and hurled himself straight at him, catching him in the midriff and bowling him over.

"Call in help," cried Holly, as she went in after Casey.

Sam gave his earpiece to Rebecca.

"You speak with Agent Jones and direct the FBI here," he told her as he jumped on the back of the fallen Russian.

"I want to handcuff this big brute before he wakes up." He quickly rummaged through his utility belt looking for a cable tie.

Holly got through the door and saw that Casey was rolling on the ground with the other man. She turned just in time to see Franco get to his feet and take off down a corridor.

"You're not getting away this time," she said through gritted teeth, as she took off after him along the corridor.

Holly had felt bad for letting Franco get away at

their first encounter and felt responsible for everything that had happened since that night at the Museum.

"A man could still be alive if it wasn't for you," she shouted as she swiped her foot at Franco's legs.

It worked; he tumbled over and over down the corridor. Before he could get up, Holly attacked, pouncing on him like a lioness going in for the kill.

She threw herself up to get maximum impact and dropped her knee deep into Franco's back.

He was already injured from his clash with the Russians and the force of the impact knocked the wind out of him.

Within moments, the place was swarming with the undercover FBI Agents.

Ivan and Halina were overhead in the helicopter and saw the commotion below. They informed General Belenov and were instructed not to take any chances and return to the yacht immediately. The Yacht set sail for International waters.

BREAKING NEWS ALERTS
more info on www.wdcnews.com

CHAPTER ELEVEN

SECRETS OF THE CRYPTEX

Later that evening, they were all back at the training camp for a debrief. The FBI had found a small satchel belonging to Franco, it contained; his false passport, the missing USB stick, and the Cryptex. The diamond wasn't amongst these items and despite a thorough search of the park it was nowhere to be seen.

Holly was the tech expert and was currently examining the files from the USB. It appeared to be instructions supplied by the Russians, on how to use the Cecret Band and Stealth Drones. She ran a software programme that she had designed to find deleted files previously stored on the USB.

The other items were lying on the table and Rebecca had picked up the Cryptex, trying to make different five letter words by aligning the alphabet wheels.

Agent Jones began his debriefing by congratulating everyone on the success of the three arrests and the seizure of the money.

"Has Franco told us where the diamond is?" Asked Sam.

"No, he's denying that he has the diamond," replied Agent Jones.

"Could it be in here," said Rebecca, as she held out the Cryptex.

"It's certainly big enough to contain the diamond and there is a possibility that it does have a chamber. However, we've put it through the x-ray machine and because it's made of Brass, we can't tell. So without the code to open it, we'll never know," said a disappointed Agent Jones.

"Can't we cut it open?" Asked Rebecca.

"We considered using a laser but there is a chance that we would end up cutting through the diamond too and we can't take that risk because it's a national treasure."

"We only have one option left," said Agent

Jones, as he looked around the room at everyone.

"What's that?" Asked Casey.

"We grant Franco complete immunity for the safe return of the diamond," he replied with sadness.

Holly couldn't believe what she was hearing.

"You mean we let him go?"

"You can't do that! Surely there must be another way." Sam quipped in.

"This has been Franco's back up plan right from the start, hasn't it?" Questioned Casey.

"Quite possibly," said Agent Jones.

A stony silence fell over the room as the realisation sunk in the Franco could walk free. Agent Jones could see the disappointment etched on each of their faces. Rebecca passed him the Cryptex as he walked to the door.

They were all aware that their main mission objective was to recover the Hope Diamond. It was not only valued at $320 million dollars but regarded as one of the world's greatest natural treasures. Despite knowing all this, Agent Jones still found it difficult accepting that he was about to offer such a prolific jewel thief his freedom.

"Wait!" Shouted Holly after him.

"Let me check something before you speak to him," as she quickly got her cell phone from her bag and began searching through her photographs for the image that she took in his apartment, the night she discovered the bag hidden beneath the floorboard.

"I think I might have it," she cried in excitement.

"What do you mean?" Asked Casey as they all gathered around her.

"The Cryptex was among the items that I found within his apartment. It's a long shot but try to open it with the combination word CURSE."

Agent Jones began turning each wheel in turn until he had matched up the letters in the right order. Gently pulling at the edge of the Cryptex, it started to open.

"You've done it Holly," he exclaimed as he turned the hidden chamber upside down to reveal the diamond.

There were screams of delight and high fives from everyone. They had done it! They had cracked the code and found the diamond, which meant that Franco was now going to jail for a very long time.

Casey suddenly grabbed Rebecca in a head lock and ruffled her hair.

"I knew I'd get you at some point," he laughed, as she shrieked and tried to break free.

The room erupted with laughter.

The next day, they were all presented with an award for their bravery and dedication in cracking the case of the Cursed Diamond. The Curator for the Natural History Museum attended the ceremony and Holly was delighted to be asked to personally return the diamond to him.

Sam and Rebecca were also presented with their Orange coloured Agent t-shirts for having successfully completed two missions.

As Rebecca stood back looking down at her t-shirt and award, she couldn't help think about Madame Le Harve and her mysterious warning. Had the Curse of the Hope Diamond been linked to Brakker's demise or was it just plain bad luck?

After the formal presentations had finished,

Casey and Holly were congratulating the other two on their new t-shirts when Agent Evans appeared by their sides.

"I have one more presentation for you all" she said to the group as she held up four VIP tickets to the Theme Park.

"When the curator of the museum heard about the events that occurred on your visit to the theme park, he thought you deserved a day off to return to the park and have some fun. So he pulled some strings and arranged a limo to take you all to the park, where you will spend the day as their special guests.

"OMG!" Squealed Rebecca "I cant wait!"

"Awesome! Does that mean we don't have to wait in queues?" Inquired an excited Sam.

"No queues and you even get to remain in the park after normal hours," replied a beaming Agent Evans.

"Get you all outside in five minutes," she added as she headed out the door.

The four Agents began chatting excitedly about what rides they wanted to go on first when an alert sounded on Holly's phone.

She stepped aside from the group to check her phone. The alert indicated that the search on Franco's USB was completed.

"I'll catch up you up in a minute. I need to look at this deleted file that I recovered on Franco's USB," shouted Holly after them all.

She was delighted that her software programme had worked and that she had managed to recover at least one deleted file from the Russian's USB, her face turned to shock when the file opened and she realised that the file made reference to a plan for a Gold Bullion Heist...

HOTELS AND RESORTS

Spy Quest is available to play at the following hotels and resorts;

America

Sheraton Vistana Resort, 8800 Vistana Centre Drive, Orlando, Florida 32821

Sheraton Vistana Villages, 12401 International Drive, Orlando, Florida 32821

The Westin Kierland Resort & Villas, 15620 North Clubgate Drive, Scottsdale, Arizona 85254

Westin Ka'anapali Ocean Resort, 6 Kai Ala Drive, Lahaina, Maui, Hawaii 96761

Westin Princeville Ocean Resort, 3838 Wyllie Road, Princeville, Kaua'i, Hawaii 96722

Westin Desert Willow Villas, 75 Willow Ridge, Palm Desert, California 92260

Westin Mission Hills Resort & Spa 71777 Dinah Shore Drive Rancho Mirage, California 92270

Sheraton Desert Oasis, 17700 North Hayden Road, Scottsdale, Arizona 85255

Vistana's Beach Club & PGA Resort, 10740 South Ocean Drive, Jensen Beach, Florida 34957

Sheraton Mountain Vista Villas, Avon / Vail Valley, CO 81620

Westin Riverfront Mountain Villas, Lakeside Terrace Resort, 160 West Beaver Creek Blvd, Avon, CO 81620

Orange Lake Resort, 8505 Irlo Bronson Memorial Highway, Kissimmee, Florida 34747

Wyndham Bonnet Creek Resort (Walt Disney World), 9560 Via Encinas, Lake Buena Vista, Florida 32830

U.S. Virgin Islands

Westin St. John Resort & Villas, 300A Chocolate Hole, St. John, U.S. Virgin Islands 00831

Mexico

Westin Lagunamar Ocean Resort, Blvd Kukulcan KM 12.5 Lote 18, Zona Hotelera, Cancun, Quintana Roo 77500, Mexico

Scotland

Crieff Hydro, Crieff, Perthshire.

Hilton Craigendarroch, Ballater.

Macdonald Aviemore Resort, Aviemore.

We are always adding resorts to our list, so check out the website for where you can play it and for the latest news about upcoming books!

Do you have what it takes to become an SQA Agent ? We'll be watching to see how you get on!